VOL. 2, NO. 2　　　　　　　　　　　　　　　　**ISSUE #6**

FEATURES

NEW STORIES

CLASSIC REPRINT

FROM THE CAT'S PERCH

Welcome to the sixth issue of *Black Cat Mystery Magazine*.

This issue is the last in which all the stories were selected by John Betancourt and Carla Coupe. Our next few issues will include stories selected by some combination of Carla, John, and me. Moving forward, I'll have more influence on content as I recently assumed sole editorship of *BCMM* while John continues as publisher.

Regular readers are already familiar with my writing, but few are familiar with my editorial background. My earliest experience includes 21 issues of the science fiction fanzine *Knights*. Since then, I've spent fourteen years editing a weekly newsletter for gardeners, fifteen years editing a monthly tabloid for seniors, and seventeen years and counting as managing editor or editor of *Texas Gardener*, a bi-monthly consumer magazine. Additionally, I've edited several crime fiction anthologies for Wildside Press and Down & Out Books, and stories from those anthologies have been short-listed for major awards and included in best-of-year anthologies.

Our goal is to publish quarterly, with three numbered issues and one special issue each year. To that end, I hope you enjoy our soon-to-be-released first special issue—*Black Cat Mystery Magazine Presents Private Eyes*.

For our regular issues, like this one, John has charged me with ensuring that *BCMM* is home to the full range of subgenres within our field, and I plan to do just that. Enjoy!

—Michael Bracken
Editor, *Black Cat Mystery Magazine*

Staff

PUBLISHER & EXECUTIVE EDITOR
John Gregory Betancourt

EDITOR
Michael Bracken

WILDSIDE PRESS SUBSCRIPTION SERVICES
Karl Würf

PRODUCTION TEAM
Sam Cooper
Steve Coupe
Shawn Garrett
Sam Hogan
Yamini Manikoth

SEVEN CARD JOKER HIGH
TREY R. BARKER

north of the line…

Daniel sipped his whiskey.
And waited.
If he got a call, there would be a package.

* * * *

south of the line…

"You find me that puta."
"Jefe, we—"
"When you find him, kill him."
"I'm not a murderer."
Jefe laughed. "You have a moral streak now?"
The man with the burned face took a steadying breath. Debt owed or not, he damn sure didn't need a lecture from this swine. Drugs north… cash and guns and plasma TVs south and none of that made this son of a bitch a man. "Probably not, but I am not a murderer."
"Find him," Jefe said. "He stole my wife. He stole my daughter."
"Yes, he did."

* * * *

between…

"Do not stop, Ysidra."
"But where are we going?"
Fleeing…so your father can't kill me for taking you. So that he can't lose you again.
"Mama?"
But mostly? Fleeing because your young girl's beauty is already maturing.
That maturity had come too soon, creeping up on Yasmin. One day, her 12-year-old daughter had suddenly slipped into the body of a 16-year-old girl. Soon the men in the village and from elsewhere would willingly mistake her for a grown woman.

"Hush, Ysidra. Do as Mommy tells you."

"Yes, ma'am."

Terror rode heavy in Yasmin's belly. Every sound scared and exhausted her. When cars passed she held her daughter on the ground, her hand covering her daughter's mouth. Her free hand she kept wrapped tightly around Ernesto's .50 caliber monster, what he called "El Pene."

Twice military jeeps had crept nearby, one staying a half hour. When the jeeps had finally gone, Yasmin laid in the dirt and cried for ten minutes.

I could go back. I could return our daughter to him. Maybe his punishment will be less a nightmare than running.

No. She would not condemn her daughter to that. She'd flee and keep her daughter safe. And when the next car or truck passed, instead of stepping into their path and returning to Ernesto, Yasmin would push them deeper into the scrub.

Which meant safer from those who searched, but it also meant farther off the line of travel she was to follow. If they wandered too far, she'd never find the right batch of broken-down, abandoned houses. If she never found those, she and Yasmin would die, either at the hands of whoever came along, or at Ernesto's hands when whoever came along took them back.

"Mama? Shouldn't we go?"

Ysidra was a strong child. No, a tough child. There was a difference. She was an oak tree in a hurricane. "Si."

Yasmin pushed them north, hoping the darkness swallowed their tracks. As they walked, dancing with scrub and rocks, Yasmin told her daughter stories of happy families and magical kingdoms where little girls grew up to be princesses.

* * * *

Except princesses didn't get lost in the desert.

They'd passed what could have once been tiny villages but were now just forgotten houses that probably served as transitory shelter for mules or coyotes or cartel-bought soldiers. None of them were the house she sought and now she was so turned around she had no idea which direction to go. She held the picture she'd been given.

"We are lost, Ysidra. I made a mistake."

"This way, Mama."

"Yeah?"

"I think." After a studious moment, Ysidra nodded. "Si."

Swallowing a ball of fear as large as the bullets in Ernesto's gun, Yasmin nodded and followed her tough child.

* * * *

north of the line…

The phone shattered the air. Like a ball-peen hammer against bone.

When Daniel answered, his connection said, "They are coming, jefe."

"Damnit. I am not jefe."

A cracked, broken laugh came back to him. "They think you are. They swear your name and whisper, 'jefe.'"

"Fuck." They'd gotten his name? He'd worked damn hard to keep his name out of this shit. "Are they coming or not?"

"Daniel, please. The men watch. You and Father William must tread lightly."

"They know the padre, too?"

"Not him specifically. They know a Daniel and a new priest. They know there is a tunnel."

Daniel rubbed his temple. "Do they know where?"

"No one knows where, Daniel. It is like the tunnel magically opened up in the desert and through it their wives and sons and daughters disappear."

Magically…seventy or eighty years ago, maybe more. It was an old tunnel, maybe an extended mining tunnel but who really knew. Daniel had found the opening just after he'd bought the property. Weeks later, he finally mustered the courage to traverse the entire thing. Chopping and hacking with a machete through decades' worth of overgrowth and dead animals. Coming out in Mexico was a ball-racking jolt, though.

"Well, whatever…. They don't scare me."

"They should."

Daniel stared at his mother's dirty and torn picture, hanging on the wall. "They have no fucking idea who I am, name or not. And they sure as hell don't know where I am."

"Tonight there will be a woman and her daughter. The daughter is very beautiful. Her father lost her in a card game…seven card joker high, they tell me. The winner did terrible things to her. When the mother objected, the father hurt her…very badly."

"They were lucky to find you."

"They are all lucky to find you, Daniel."

Maybe, but there weren't enough savable victims to keep the visions of his own dead mother out of his head; not enough bathtub whiskey to keep those visions bound and gagged behind the locked door of memory.

"Be careful. The men are angry. Even the military patrols now."

"They won't find anything," Daniel said.

Stuffing his pistol and some cash into his pocket, Daniel hung up and went outside. He owned better than 100 acres, bordered along the Rio Grande river, with Rio Grande City 25 or so miles south, Roma a bit closer, U.S. Route 83 closer still. It was all scrub; valueless to most people. To him the value was in how the morning sun burned the air golden and how the delicate night breeze cooled both skin and soul. This valley was his mother's land, and when he'd retired and bought the ranch, he'd lovingly moved her from the cemetery in McAllen to this place. He'd faced her east because she loved the morning sun best.

"I miss you, Mama."

Then Daniel hopped on his battered ATV and headed for the tunnel entrance, hidden deep on his property.

* * * *

north of the line…

"I am Daniel."

Not his real name and he never offered even a fake last name.

"I am Yasmin. This is Ysidra. My daughter."

Daniel gave the pair a soft smile. "She is beautiful."

Yasmin's eyes burned, loaded with traces of violence. She pulled the girl close.

"I meant no offense. Father William will be here soon. He will take you north."

"Padre Patrick?"

"He's gone." Two months gone and no one knew why, though Daniel had seen the stress of smuggling abused women and children to safety in the crevices of his face. "Father William is a good man."

"Where?"

Daniel shrugged. A sanctuary city; San Francisco, Chicago, maybe Indianapolis. Some place desperate in its anonymity.

They climbed aboard the ATV and headed toward his house. Daniel would feed them, make sure they had a few dollars, and wait for Father William to take them. Then Daniel would go to bed. Tomorrow morning, he'd get up, work on his new birdbath, and maybe, in a few days, there'd be another family.

Over a cold meal of chicken, his guests said little. They were scared, Daniel knew, and embarrassed. Though they knew they weren't the only ones in this situation, most mothers were embarrassed for allowing themselves to get into this situation. Embarrassed to be victims.

"My mother was a victim. So was I. And I'm still embarrassed."

'Cause I ran away from it all.

Daniel nodded toward his mother's picture. "He killed her. Beat her when he was drunk. He was always drunk. He came after me and she got between us. He killed her and I hustled on the streets."

Yasmin held the chicken halfway to her mouth. "Great story. Very uplifting. Gracias."

Ysidra giggled.

"Yeah…sorry. Bad choice."

So he told a different story. His mother and him at the zoo in B'ville and eating ice cream at a summer play staged in a park in McAllen and splashing in the reservoir. In a few minutes, he and Ysidra were laughing and Yasmin was smiling, though her eyes were still hooded and scared and angry.

Because she came from violence. Husbands who were cartel members, soldiers of those dealers, policemen or politicians, sometimes teachers, oftentimes doctors. Always respectable men who, regardless of the public sheen, had violence in common. A tendency to use fists to express love and devotion.

"My mother's name was Monita," Daniel said.

"She was a good woman?" Yasmin said.

"Yes."

* * * *

south of the line…

"You have a man ready?"

"Si."

"This side of the river?"

"This side, that side; the border does not matter." Jefe laughed. "There is no border."

"I will send you to a house."

"And I will kill him. Where is the tunnel?"

The man kept his voice even. "His grands had some land far above Piedras Negras."

"Two hundred miles away?"

"Maybe more. Daniel's going to hide that tunnel somewhere far away, Jefe. Trust me on this. I found him for you, didn't I?"

"Si."

"So we're good? No more debt?"

"No more debt. But you'll be back."

"Fuck that. I'm done with your bullshit."

"Once a man's gotten a taste…."

"I have other tastes now, Jefe."

"I will see you again."

Into Jefe's heavy laugh, the man hung up the phone.

* * * *

north of the line…

Four hours later, Father William arrived.

"You'll come with me," he said. "For a few hours. Then a driver'll take you."

And they'd disappear into the expanse of America.

Just like Daniel's mother had tried to do. She'd been lower-middle class from Monterrey while his father had teethed in dives all over Ireland before traveling to Mexico to work oil rigs. They stumbled upon each other and a quick bar hook-up had led to twelve years of violence. When she was finally done, she and Daniel fled north, only to be found near McAllen. Drunk, his father had raged about a man's rights. Daniel had been sober and scared and had stood up.

"Gonna be a man now?" his father had said, his fists hard and heavy from working the rigs.

Howling, Monita had gone at her husband mercilessly, gouging her nails into his eyes and cheeks until blood flowed freely. They spun and twisted, physical manifestations of swirling desert dust storms.

Panicked, Daniel had run for help; up and down dirty country roads, pleading for someone to call la policia. But the quiet houses, spread out on half-acres of land sold as post-urban "country living," stayed quiet.

No one called and when he returned ten minutes later, his father was forever gone and his mother was dead.

"How go the repairs?" Daniel asked.

Father William sighed. "Too slow. But the rectory'll be fixed soon enough, I guess." The man snapped his fingers. "Like there was no damage at all. I think—" Father William grabbed Daniel's arm. "Who the hell is that?"

A man emerged from the darkness; his walk stooped beneath the weight of his backpack. He stopped near Daniel's deck. "Agua?"

Father William quickly gave the man a bottle. Father William had spent years working the passageways along Arizona's "Devil's Highway." He routinely carried extra water and food.

Sitting heavily, the man drank with great urgency.

"Tired?" Daniel asked.

"Been walking awhile, hombre." He wiped his face with a tattered rag from his pack.

"Ladies, go inside." Daniel nodded toward his door. "Father, go with them."

"What?"

"Go."

When they were gone, Daniel said, "Mule?"

Smirking, the man shrugged.

"I saw the gun."

"Did you?"

"You wanted me to."

"Just trying to get down the road, hombre. Need a little help to make that trip easier. Gotta carry a gun out here. Coyotes and cartel soldiers and local cops...everybody's on the steal."

Daniel yanked his pistol from his waistband. "Get outta here, asshole."

The man raised his hands slowly. "Careful, hombre, you don't want to hurt nobody."

"You sure? Been looking to hurt somebody for a while."

"Yeah?" The man stood. "You got some fight? Gotta protect them girls? The priest, too?"

Daniel thumbed the hammer.

"Easy... I've met him before. I go back and forth sometimes."

"Mule."

This time, the smile seemed genuine. "Trying to get by."

"Try getting outta here."

"You ain't so neighborly."

Daniel shoved the barrel against the man's forehead. "How's that? Better?"

"Whoa, hombre."

The man moved slowly, as though he didn't want Daniel to mistake anything he did. Instead of slinging his pack over his shoulder, he carried it in front of him.

"Don't ever let me catch you on my property again... hombre."

The man offered an apologetic smile. "Anything you say...."

It was the smile. That split second when Daniel watched the man's face rather than his hands.

"Anything you say… jefe."

The gun materialized seemingly from nowhere. The air split with shots, deadening Daniel's hearing. Great gouts of orange flame tore from the barrel. A shot hammered his arm while another split the air at his head.

"You wanna take our women?" the man said.

Warm blood spilling down his arm, Daniel yelped and fell sideways. His own gun suddenly seemed so inadequate. He fired and fired, had no idea what, if anything he hit.

"The fuck you think you are… hombre?"

Bullets peppered the dirt, kicking clods into Daniel's legs. His own bullets seemed to hit nothing. His shots were like dogs barking. Little yips that might not actually hurt anyone.

But then a dog barked louder. Huge, racking barks that scared Daniel and sent the man fleeing into the dark. The dog barked two or three times after him.

Behind him, Yasmin held a gigantic gun. It leaked white smoke. "He came to kill us."

Daniel nodded, pressed a hand to his bloody arm.

"My husband sent him."

"Maybe. There are a lotta pissed off husbands."

"You have stolen that many wives and children?"

He headed back to the house. "My way of fighting back, I guess."

"Against?"

Finally, when they stood on the back porch, his mother's grave visible in the moonlight, he said, "My father's fists."

She kissed him on the cheek and went inside. Less than twenty minutes later, Father William, Yasmin, and Ysidra were gone. Daniel settled back with a bandage and whiskey.

* * * *

south of the line…

"Sure, I know where they went. Your man fucked it up. Should have hired smarter."

"Hired you?"

"No. I'm not… I'm not a murderer, I keep telling you that."

"You do keep telling me that. But remember this: licking the white and drinking the agave juice can lead a man to desperate places. Tell me…what are your other tastes?"

"Fuck off, asshole."

"Careful, you still have debt."

"My debt was done in our last phone call. Your idiot soldiers are not my problem."

"I wonder at your motives."

"None of your business, Jefe. I'm not looking to deal. I'm not smuggling iron or cash. You and I have no competition."

"Because your tastes are…more base than drugs and guns and cash?"

The man sighed. "You have no idea."

* * * *

north of the line…

Two hours later, Daniel was awakened by someone banging on his door. Panicked, he grabbed his pistol, moaned at the slow burn in his arm, and peeked through a window. Yasmin stood on his porch, crying and covered in black paint.

His breath stopped. It wasn't paint.

He knew they'd found him.

"Yasmin. What happened?"

Snot covered her lips, and tears had cut harsh, jagged lines through the dirt on her face. She shoved him backward into the house and slammed the door. Eventually, she was able to tell him. "Father William is dead."

Daniel had known it. The moment he saw her covered in blood. "Where is Ysidra?"

She collapsed to the couch. "He has her."

"Who?"

"My husband, damnit. He sent someone. The man who was here shooting."

"Your husband lost her in a card game…. Why would he want her back?"

Yasmin glared. "He wants his property back."

Daniel paced his living room, gun in hand. If her father had her taken, she was long since back on the south side. He eyed Yasmin. "They didn't kill you."

Her glare intensified. "You think I did this? You think I am somehow part of this?"

"I don't— I didn't mean—"

"He came with another man. His face was…scarred. Maybe burned." She looked away, as though searching the inside of her head. "He seemed so familiar, the scarred man." She took a deep breath. "They came into the rectory. They killed Father William." Her shoulders arched and her back straightened. "I killed one of them."

For a moment, a split-second of a heartbeat, Yasmin was Daniel's mother. Standing in front him, covered in blood and snot, battered but violently triumphant. This—killing to protect her young—was what Daniel had always secretly wanted his mother to do. That she had tried and failed kept him awake deep into every night of his soul. But the fantasy, what cradled him to sleep, was that she had succeeded.

"The second one grabbed Ysidra. He put a gun to her head. He took her from me."

Daniel shook his head. "I'm sorry, Yasmin, but I can't get her back from Mexico. If he has her, then it is too late for her."

"She is not in Mexico."

Daniel stopped. "What? Where is she?"

"In your tunnel."

The silence was a hangman's noose. Absolutely she was in the tunnel. This all started with, and in, that tunnel. It had to end there.

"My husband wants his property, but more he wants the man who stole his property."

Fifty years ago, Daniel had run. The memory was as fresh and sticky as road tar in high summer. He had run from his father while his mother's screams pierced his ears. He'd believed he was running to find help. Now he knew that was bullshit and the guilt shamed him. He hadn't been running to the police or for her. He'd been running for himself. To survive. To come out of his father's shit storm alive.

It was why he had run most every day since then, too.

Hustling the streets of south Texas for ten years led him to a low-level sales job, which led him, eventually, to a multi-national corporation that paid him to run away in first class airline seats and across the oceans on anonymous liners. In twenty-three years with that company, he'd requested postings to seventeen different regional offices around the world.

But every moment had pointed him toward this night.

He should have seen the violence coming when he'd started this mess months ago.

Be honest, Daniel, you did. In fact, you courted it. Saving women and children from some of the most violent men in the Americas? And doing it within spitting distance of their homes?

Maybe he had wanted this battle. Maybe he had wanted an opportunity to finish the standing up he'd started outside of McAllen with a drunken father.

Yasmin put her hands on his chest. They burned with fire. "Please, Daniel. He says they just want to talk. They'll give my daughter back."

Tears, as fresh as the blood on her shirt, lined her face.

"They lie. They are machismo. They don't want to talk. They want to kill me."

She shook her head vehemently. "No, Daniel, they just want to—"

"Shhhhh. They want to kill." He gave her a long hug and went to his ATV. "So do I."

* * * *

between...

He found Ysidra in the tunnel. Bound with rope, gagged with duct tape. Her hair, so beautiful in the moonlight hours earlier, was disheveled and astray like a dirty, lost puppy. Playing his flashlight over her, her fear ratcheted up with every step he took. When he was still thirty or forty feet away, she pissed herself and began to cry.

"Shit. Ysidra, I'm so sorry." He yanked the flashlight around so she could see his face. When she did, she started laughing; a rusty, hysterical sound that tightened his throat. "We're getting outta here, don't worry."

She stopped laughing and in the silence he heard...nothing.

His throat dried. If they were here to bargain, they'd be here. Anything else meant they were looking to simply kill them both.

"Everything'll be fine, Ysidra."

He pawed at the ropes, snugly tied around her hips and breasts, between her legs. How she was tied wasn't just ropes holding her immobile. That would have been around her ankles, maybe her calves. Hands behind her back. This was completely different.

This was—Daniel gagged in the back of his throat—fun, maybe?

"Damnit."

Ysidra tried to speak through the tape. Daniel pulled it off as gently as he could.

"Daniel." Her voice was a hoarse whisper. "It was the priest."

"Father William?" Confusion ran with the sweat on Daniel's face. "He's dead."

"No. The other priest. Father Patrick."

Daniel's stomach rolled. He'd not talked to the priest since the man had left without a word. Daniel's assumption was that Father Patrick could no longer handle the psychic toll of smuggling humans to safety.

Maybe that assumption had been wrong.

"How do you know Father Patrick?"

She snapped her mouth closed, her eyes toward the ground.

"Ysidra? How do you know Father Patrick?"

"He…. He plays cards."

"Yeah. Poker. He likes seven card."

"The joker is the high card. That rule drives my daddy crazy."

"Ysidra?"

"He plays cards with my father. He usually wins."

A long silence filled the gap between them. Daniel's heart broke for this little girl. He hugged her, the ropes be damned, and hated that she was stiff and resistant.

"And your mother had to get you back."

Ysidra nodded.

Far along the tunnel, toward Mexico, they heard footsteps. Two men talking cautiously.

"Hurry, Daniel, untie me. Hurry."

Daniel shut everything out. The footsteps behind them, the way the ropes had been tied, the smell of the smoke and fire in the rectory that waffled up from his memory. He worked feverishly to untie her. His fingers fumbled with fear and adrenaline. The knots weren't complicated, but his sweaty skin made it almost impossible to get a grip. He pushed and pulled and eventually the ropes began to loosen.

"What the fuck?"

Daniel whirled. He yanked his gun and held it in front of him, a talisman. "Who the hell is that?"

"Who the hell is you?" one of the men said.

Beneath Daniel's flashlight, they were impossibly skinny and delicate. Not muscled-up thugs at all. They were scared, their mouths tight and eyes wide. Their hands hovered near their guns, but they made no move.

Daniel had almost expected to see Father Patrick. "I'm taking her. Try and stop me and I'll kill you. Choice is yours."

"I don't give no fuck 'bout no girl. You neither. We came to pick up a package."

The second said to Ysidra, "Unless you is the package."

Her face was defiant, her hands curled to fists.

"There is no package," Daniel said.

"Then ain't neither of you walking," the first man said. "And I ain't dying…not today."

"Where is Patrick?"

Ysidra stepped out of the ropes.

"Who?"

The second one shook his head, his broken-down cowboy hat, a skull and crossbones holding the hatband in place, bobbing with the move. "Don't know no Patrick."

"Bullshit." Daniel ground his teeth. "Don't screw with me."

They were only eight or ten feet from Daniel. Close enough to smell them. Stale booze, sweat, violence, the indolent reek of arrogance.

The smell of his father.

Daniel flicked the safety, thumbed the hammer back.

"No, no, hombre," the second one said. "Jefe wants to talk. Wants to make a deal for your tunnel."

Daniel shook his head. "No."

"Some drugs, some guns, maybe some whores, no problem."

"Big problem. Not in my tunnel."

The first one, the talker of the two, grinned. "Your tunnel? How about this, gringo? How about we kill you and take your tunnel?" He eyed Ysidra. "And your woman."

Daniel had fired his pistol before. Cans and wood, at targets on a range, even at a coyote or two stalking him when he camped out. But somehow he'd expected more, as though if the gun splashed a man's head all over a wall, it would be louder.

The man went down, half his face gone, the other half surprised. His body crumpled, a bit of waste paper tossed into the garbage.

"Whoa." The man held his hands out. "Don't wanna be dead. Hold on."

Again, Daniel watched the smile rather than the hands.

Again, he was caught short.

The man fired and dove to the side of the tunnel. Daniel emptied his magazine. Ysidra ran. Daniel saw her, peripherally, and wanted to run with her. Wanted to feel the ground beneath his feet, like he had when he was twelve and running from his father.

Instead, he jammed a second magazine into the pistol and kept firing. The man shot in return, bullets like hot rain. A hard fist smashed Daniel in the shin and pain exploded.

"I got'choo." The man's voice was a howl of glee. "You'll be dead. I— Fuck!"

One of Daniel's bullets found him. Then another and a third. Slowly, as though unsure of what to do next, the man slid to the ground.

"We'll both be dead, asshole," Daniel said. "You ready? I am."

"Fuck yooooooou, hombre."

Daniel fired again just as another fist smashed his chest. When he looked at himself, he almost laughed. It looked like black paint, like someone had splashed him for a prank. Around him, the air had chilled suddenly, as though a frozen breeze was blasting through the tunnel.

Then as quickly as a heartbeat, the shooting was finished. The man, broken on the ground, was silent and in the harsh glow of a dying flash-light, Daniel saw him staring. His watery brown eyes stayed on Daniel, even as his mouth moved silently.

When Daniel fell, unable to keep his legs under him, he found himself at eye level with the man he'd killed. They stared at each other for what seemed like hours.

"Gonna be a man now?" the man asked, his voice that of Daniel's father.

"I'm standing up."

"Fuck you…you killed me." The man's face pinched.

After the man was dead, and after his own pain had subsided into memories of his mother, Daniel closed his eyes.

* * * *

north of the line…

Patty sipped tequila and dealt himself a hand of seven card joker high.

And waited. If there was a phone call, there would be a package.

They were all dead. Father William and Daniel's contact across the river, Yasmin when she returned to the rectory to wait for the bogus deal Patty had floated, the two men Patty had sent to retrieve Ysidra. Ysidra had slipped away but that was fine. Patty would never see her again but he'd had her already and there were so many others.

Above all, Daniel was dead.

Patty threw back a blast of tequila and banged a hand against the table.

Daniel had been a self-righteous assfuck, so lost in the failures of his past that he painted everyone else with the brush of those failures.

"We're all human, Daniel," Patty said to no one. "We all have flaws."

He sat on Daniel's deck, waiting for the phone call.

"But not all of us are afflicted with the pain of those flaws."

He also waited for the first of his ventures to come through the tunnel.

Jefe was searching high above Piedras Negras for a tunnel, if he was searching at all. His routes were secure and vital, he needed no new routes, and the man who'd stolen his property was dead.

The phone rang.

"There are four, Patty. Very beautiful."

"Not from around here, right?"

"Two from Belize, two further south than that."

"Let them come, then."

Patty hung up. Drank his tequila. Played his cards.

Since 1994, Trey R. Barker has published more than 300 short stories. He started in horror but now works predominantly in crime; with the occasional hard turn into just about every other genre, including poetry about serial killers. He's published ten novels and assorted other books, and spent nearly two decades drifting into and out of, and back into, the world of journalism.

THE LOSER

ROBERT GUFFEY

Ernesto walked the wheel through his hands, jackknifing into the fast lane, as the sound of the helicopter drew nearer. The blades sliced through smog-filled air, so damn close, as if the pilot were planning to land on the roof of the van. Behind him, police sirens wailed. On either side of the speeding van, cars slowed down and pulled away from him, frightened. That gave him a little bit of satisfaction—just a little bit. Few people in this life had ever been afraid of him.

The 405 was a crazy obstacle course of glass and metal death machines, all of them pissed off and frustrated that their ride home from some pitiful job in an office somewhere in downtown L.A. was being disrupted by a kid in a stolen vehicle. Were they listening to the news reports on the radio? Did they know his name?

An asshole in an SUV cut in front of him, trying to play hero. Son of a bitch. Ernesto didn't slow down; he sped up. Fuck, why should he care? The van wasn't even his. He scraped the side of the SUV, ripping off the asshole's rearview mirror with a shrieking, crippling collision. He got so close, he could see the look of confused terror in the face of the beefy white dude behind the wheel. Fuck you, cowboy. That's a mighty bad moustache you've got there. Have fun fixing the entire right side of your gas guzzler, shithead.

Jesus. At least *that* was satisfying. The cars ahead of him parted like the Red Sea in that cheesy old Charlton Heston movie his grandmother forced him to watch every Easter.

I guess they didn't want their precious cars destroyed like shithead's back there. Good thinking. That should make things a little easier.

He'd watched crazy scenes like this a billion times on the news. You couldn't get through a week of L.A. TV without some jackball losing his shit over an unfaithful girlfriend or some useless crap like that; suddenly, the dude freaks out on the freeway, lashes out on some stranger while deadlocked around LAX, then caps it off by leading the CHP on an insane chase all over the South Bay before getting his tires blown out by metal spikes laid down on the concrete. Inevitably, the dude would be dragged out of his own car by some joyboys with a loaded .38 and a couple of hard-ons and his balls ripped to shreds by the canine corps. All for what? 'Cause somebody flipped him off on the freeway? 'Cause his bitch wouldn't suck him off the night before? Ernesto always thought those dudes were chumps.

Never in a million years did he imagine he would become one of them. This had not been a good day, oh not at all.

But now that he was trapped in this situation, he was determined not to end up like all the others. What did he have to lose?

Think, Ernesto, think. There has to be some way out of this....

He thought about the dead body jostling around in the back seat. He thought about the revolver, the one with only five bullets in the chamber, sliding back and forth across the dash. He thought about his girlfriend, who finally agreed to have sex with him for the first time the night before. He'd never had sex before. God, he'd been wanting to fuck that bitch since he was fifteen. He'd been dating her for two years. He *deserved* her cherry, after all that time and money he invested in her. And she agreed, and she took her panties off for him, and they fucked in the back seat of his brother's beat-up Oldsmobile. It only lasted a few seconds, but what the hell. At least he wasn't a virgin anymore. At least he could die knowing that.

Man, Ernesto, what the fuck are you thinking? You're not gonna die. Think... Think about the dude's wallet, the one you slipped in your pocket... Think about the cards... The cards...

Ernesto knew exactly where he had to go. It wasn't that far from here. They wouldn't be expecting it at all.

Ernesto took a deep breath and stepped on the gas, increased his speed all the way up to 90... 100... 110....

He reached out for the dash, flipped on the radio, expecting to hear a news broadcast prominently discussing his background, interviews with his friends and family, but there was nothing. Was it too soon? Not a big enough story? Perhaps tomorrow...after he was dead....

Fuck you, Ernesto. You're not going to die. You're not going to—

Ernesto slammed on the horn, pulled the van to the right, swerved around a teetering truck carrying flammable substances that just barely got out of his way. Hell, *that* would've been interesting. Five or six pigs behind him would've been caught in that blow-up. Would've been nice. A dead pig is a good pig. But that ain't worth *him* dying too, no way. Not when *he* could live instead. A free man....

Suddenly, he jackknifed to the left, took the Torrance off-ramp, barreled onto Crenshaw Blvd., slammed into the side of an orange Volkswagen bug and sent it careening into a station wagon filled with screaming kids, burned rubber past the Mobil oil refinery, the one that was always exploding and releasing poisonous gas into the air. Ernesto hated Torrance. He and his friends used to take a bus down to Torrance just to mug people. A few wallets later, they'd hop back onto the bus and return to their own neighborhood in Wilmington. The two cities weren't that far apart, and yet they were like two different worlds. Parts of Torrance looked like a white man's paradise, little gingerbread houses and white picket fences, yapping dogs in the front yard, a fat dude with a moustache barbecuing meat on a grill for the kiddies, and pleasant noxious fumes polluting their air. Oh, well. The price you have to pay to live in paradise. He always got treated like shit when he went to Torrance, so when he and Julio got old enough to steal, Ernesto said to him, "Fuck Wilmington. Nobody here's got money. Let's go to Torrance instead. You got ninety cents for the bus?" Between the two of 'em they scraped up the money. And it was the best ninety cents they'd spent in their life. They came back with a hundred and fifty bucks.

Ernesto spent his share on food. There wasn't much of it at home, not these days, ever since Mom lost her day job….

Mom. He was never gonna see her again. He knew that now.

What the fuck? It was probably better that way. He'd never been nothin' more than a burden to her. She'd be glad to see him go.

He turned up the radio as he sped through a red light. No mention of him at all. Were they totally incompetent? Wasn't he a hazard to public safety? Didn't they have to warn somebody?

The news was all cluttered up with trivia from the Middle East. Israel was bombing Lebanon again. A hundred-eighty Lebanese dead. What the fuck did that mean to him? He switched the radio to some music.

She Wants Revenge blasted out of the speakers as he swerved onto Torrance Blvd. "*I want to fucking tear you apart!*" God damn he hated that song, but it was better than silence. As he made the curve, just barely avoiding some young white chick pushing a stroller into the crosswalk, the loaded revolver shot off the dash and slammed into the car door. "Oh, shit!" he shouted. The gun slid onto the carpet between the door and the driver's seat; he couldn't see it anymore. Ernesto's heart was beating in his throat. It felt like it was going to burst out of his chest. He didn't want to see that damn piece of metal ever again. He was scared of it. Jesus, he was so glad it hadn't gone off accidentally when it hit the door.

Forget it. Don't think about it…about the first time he ever laid eyes on the damn thing…about anything that had happened today…just keep going….

* * * *

Ernesto woke up feeling pretty good. He was a man now. Margarita had spread her legs for him last night. Worked out perfectly. He'd remembered to pull out and ejaculate on her stomach, just like his older brother told him to do. "If you're havin' sex with that bitch you better pull your dick out before you come 'cause you don't want to get that cunt pregnant with a gash gremlin. Got it?" He could always rely on his brother to tell him what he needed to know, straight from the hip. What would he do without his big brother?

He and his brother had shared the same room for years. Alex often kicked him out to have sex with his girlfriends. For the past five years he'd been doing this, and sometimes Ernesto would sit out in the hall and listen to his brother have sex, the grunting and the moaning and the whispers and the screams, and afterwards his brother would shame him, make him feel like half a man because Ernesto hadn't convinced his chick to let him slip his dick inside her cunt yet, and sometimes that got Ernesto real fuckin' mad and he'd take it out on Margarita, and that was bad, and he knew that, but that didn't stop him from doing it. His girlfriend said she didn't like it when a guy begged, it was so pathetic, but he couldn't help it, and hell it finally worked, didn't it?

And now it was morning and he was feeling pretty good about himself. The sun was just rising. He liked getting up this early. Always had. Alex was still sleeping. He'd be sleeping till noon.

Ernesto grabbed his backpack and got out of the house before anyone was even up. His mom had been out of work for months, so she didn't get up till noon either. He walked down to the bus stop and waited for the first bus of the day, the one that would take him all the way to the pier in Redondo Beach. He liked to explore the South Bay on his own. He'd been doing it since he was twelve or thirteen. He didn't understand why the other kids in his neighborhood were so scared to leave their block. The rest of L.A. was accessible by bus for only a couple of dollars. His friends seemed intimidated by the white neighborhoods, but Ernesto was fascinated by them. They had no right to keep him out. If he could afford the ninety-cent bus fare to get him there, he had as much a right to be there as anyone else.

He liked to prowl around the streets of Manhattan Beach, Redondo Beach, Hermosa, Venice, Santa Monica, even the hills of Palos Verdes.

Sometimes the cops hassled him, but he wasn't doing anything wrong. He just stood his ground. He refused to feel guilty for no reason at all.

The Torrance #3, its dirty red and white paint peeling off the side, pulled up to the bus stop. Ernesto dropped his change into the glass and metal machine at the front, then went and took his usual seat in the far-right corner, way in the back. There were a lot of people on the bus, even this early. Everyone was always so quiet. Everybody was middle aged, going to work at 5:00 in the morning, dead stares in their eyes, not even reading newspapers. Just watching the ugly scenery go by.

Ernesto never realized how ugly the scenery was until he started visiting all the other cities that surrounded him. From his birth to the age of twelve he had very rarely left the city of Wilmington, much less his block. A couple of times his parents had saved up the money to take the family on a vacation to Disneyland. But they had to take the bus there. Through downtown L.A. And he remembered feeling scared of the people milling around the dirty city. It was even dirtier and scarier than Wilmington. Disneyland was a dream, but he didn't get to go there often. Just too expensive. And ever since his dad took off, there was no extra money for anything, not even for food, not really....

According to Ernesto's driver's license, he weighed 140 pounds and was 6'1". He ate what he could, when it came his way. Most of the time he ate dinner over at Margarita's house. He was ashamed of that. Ashamed of his clothes. Ashamed of the way he looked. Ashamed of the disapproving stares in the eyes of Margarita's parents. Her parents had been married for years, over twenty. That was so strange. Ernesto didn't know anyone else on the planet who had been married that long. They were very Catholic, very protective of their daughter. Ernesto wore a cross around his neck, but he didn't really believe in God. He just wore it 'cause he knew Margarita's parents would respect him a little more.

It seemed to him, and he could be wrong, but it seemed to him that nobody on this entire bus got any respect. And it was grinding them down. Every day, they woke up at 4:00 in the morning, got dressed, made a little sack lunch for themselves maybe, put on their make-up, their freshly ironed slacks, went outside to wait for a bus in the cold, and all for what? So they could report to a cash register, a little cubicle somewhere? Often he'd see middle-aged men in suits and ties riding the bus. That always confused him. What was the point? To have all the responsibilities of a rich man, but none of the rewards? He always wondered what their stories were. Recently divorced? Was it a new job, and they were just now climbing out of the hole? Or did they make so little money at their important suit-and-tie job that they couldn't afford a car? Were they angry as they sat there on the bus? Did they think it was unfair, to have to sit there side by side with dirty Wilmington scum like Ernesto? It was impossible to tell, because these people rarely had any expression on their face except for a kind of dull, numb acceptance of the day that lay ahead. Ernesto hoped he would never have that kind of look on his face.

But what if Margarita wanted to marry him? Have kids with him? Wouldn't he need to get a job just to keep her around? Was she worth it? Was anything worth that look on your face at 5:00 in the morning?

Anyway, he didn't have to deal with it right now. He didn't have to think about it. He was free. Free to do whatever the fuck he wanted. This was his celebration.

He rode the bus from Wilmington, into Carson, then Torrance, then Redondo Beach. It always amazed him how much the scenery could change in only thirty minutes. Ernesto's apartment in Wilmington was right next to a chemical factory that spewed dirt-like particles into the air day after day. On the bus, when he was going from Wilmington to Long Beach, he would try to do his homework, but as he passed by the plant tiny black particles would appear on his pure white notebook paper. And he'd have to brush it away with his palm. He always wondered, Am I breathin' that shit in?

Huge pyramid-shaped piles of sulfur, fluorescent piss-yellow, three stories high, had been dumped in the middle of the plant. It was so high, you could see it from the street. He always wondered what happened to that shit when it rained. Did it just stay there, or did some of it ever blow away? They never covered it up with nothin'. It always just sat there like a giant alien creature, watching everything that went on around it....

Immense billboards in Spanish littered every corner, almost all of them advertising alcohol. Porno shops with pink stucco walls and no windows. Iron bars on every first-floor window. Bars on the screen doors. Trash carpeting the sidewalks like makeshift rugs. White men in police cars occasionally busting a homeboy on the street corner, just outside Wilmington High. That's where the kids liked to gather, right by the homemade paper banner for The Colts, the home team, and sometimes things got rowdy and the apartment buildings next door would complain, and the cops would come. That's the only time he ever saw the cops in his neighborhood, except when somebody was murdered. The cops never prevented crime. They always just showed up afterwards to clean up the mess and identify the remains and take a lot of notes. They were like janitors, but not as friendly.

That was Ernesto's neighborhood. For the first decade of his life he had known nothing else. Then, one day, he hopped on a bus. And was amazed. Revelation. The cities surrounding him were not so far away, easily accessible, and yet they were like different worlds. Alternate dimensions living side by side. Carson wasn't too different from Wilmington. Maybe a little bit better...just a little bit. Not as many iron bars on the windows. Not as much trash in the street. The first time he saw Carson, Ernesto thought, I wish I could live here. Then he saw Torrance. Parts of it looked like Carson. Then, rapidly, things changed. Suddenly, he was in the suburbs with nice houses and pretty lawns and white children playing on the sidewalk and no trash anywhere and cops all over the place, watching. And then he was in Redondo Beach and Ernesto couldn't believe it. Why was the *sky* so much different here? How could that be? The sky here was bright blue. The air was clean. There were some days when Ernesto honestly thought Wilmington was on another planet. He'd go from one city to the other, and the sky would shift from gray to blue, just like that. From black particles clinging to your notebook to the pure salty ocean breeze.

And then came the other cities: Manhattan Beach, Hermosa, Venice, Santa Monica. Each of them a welcome refuge from the continual chaos brewing at home. Ever since Dad took off, things hadn't been so good. Fuck, it hadn't been so good when Dad was around, but at least he was bringing food home. And his mom was always on him to get a job and help out. Why? Why should I? Why isn't Dad doing that? Where is he?

His mom never had an answer to that.

So instead he'd spend his days studying all the people in the white neighborhoods, wishing he was one of them. Sometimes he'd bring his best friend Julio with him, and that's when they'd mug the little old ladies and the older dudes who looked like they had money. And in this way Ernesto began to contribute. His mom never asked where he got the money from. He never bothered to tell her.

But he only mugged people with Julio. Never alone.

He and Julio...they were brothers. Not by flesh, but by blood. Julio was always watching action movies, all kinds of action movies. Even black and white ones. He showed Ernesto one where these two guys became brothers by cutting each other's palms with a knife and mingling their blood together. So Julio insisted he and Ernesto do this late one night, out in an old baseball field grown over with weeds. It hurt like a bitch, but afterwards Julio said, "We're brothers now. Now we need to swear to die for each other." And they did.

Ernesto felt so close to Julio, he didn't even drop him as a friend when he walked in on him making moves on Margarita at this party. He watched Julio put his hand on her left breast, watched him trying to kiss her. Margarita even seemed to be getting into it. Who knows how far it would've gone if he hadn't walked in on them right then and there? They were both drunk, so Ernesto forgave them. He was mad at first, but he got over it. Ernesto saw how Julio looked at Margarita all the time, but he knew Julio would never cross that line again. Julio had apologized. They were partners in crime. Brothers to the end. Just like in the movies....

Ernesto was too scared to mug people alone. That wasn't even the main reason he visited these neighborhoods, little paradises like Redondo Beach. He came because he just wanted to get away from his life for a little while and pretend he was someone else.

Sometimes the bus was too slow for him. That's when he started hitchhiking. His mother said she and Dad used to hitchhike all the time back in the late '60s. Wearing nothing but a bikini and sandals, or shorts and sandals, she and her friends would stick their thumb out on Pacific Coast Highway and get rides all the way to the beach and back again. Nobody ever harmed them or were scared of them. Everything changed in Southern California when the Manson murders happened. You couldn't trust anybody these days, she said. Ernesto barely knew who Manson was and really didn't care. He just wanted to turn the clock back and recapture that kind of freedom.

So he started hitchhiking. Out of necessity. The Torrance buses only ran so long, until about nine o'clock at night. If you wanted to stay out later, you either had to call a cab or hitch a ride. Well, he sure as hell couldn't afford a cab. So that's when he started hitching. Sometimes people looked at him funny, and sped past him, but the people who did stop were always nice. A few of them were even white. He hadn't had any problems, not at all. He thought his mom was just being paranoid. So he never told her about it. It was his secret, something he usually did only when he was alone.

The #3 reached the Redondo Beach pier just before seven. It was bitter, freezing cold here. He was glad he brought his black jacket with him; he zipped it all the way up to his chin and went down to the shore. He watched the early morning sun spread out across the lightening sky, tossed rocks into the ocean, then bought a $1.50 churro from an Asian girl in a booth—part of his earnings from the last time he and Julio had gone out "shopping" in this neighborhood. He spent a couple of hours strolling up and down the empty beach, then decided he wanted to check out the scene in Venice.

The Venice Boardwalk was always cool. There were always insane white people there, crazed old hippies standing on wooden benches, giving speeches about bullshit. About the war in Iraq. About the CIA doing this and that. How they were behind the illegal drug trade and other paranoid crap. Jesus, if so, at least they were doing something right. Drugs had always been good to Ernesto. Sometimes he'd buy a twenty bag from his brother and sell it for a profit in Venice. You could always make good money on that shit on the Boardwalk, no doubt about it, way more than he could in Wilmington. If his mother knew what he was up to she'd freak, but so what? It's not like he was doing it all the time. Not as much as the CIA, right? Right.

Ernesto sat on the soft sand, watching a couple of white teenagers, only a few years older than him, making out on the sand not far from where the waves were coming in. Sometimes he brought Margarita out here with him, but not often. This was his own private paradise. Not even Julio came with him to the beach. He liked to just sit here and think. About his dad. About his mom. School. Just nonsense. Maybe next time, though, he'd bring her out here with him. Maybe this is where he'd propose to her.

Aw, fuck, man, what the hell're you thinking? You saw what Dad did to Mom. You want to end up like that? That's crazy talk. Get your ass out of here and go to Venice and make some money.

He had a twenty bag in his jacket. He could unload it on some old hippie and make this a business trip. Why not? He got up from the sand and wandered back to the bus stop. He glanced over his shoulder at the couple on the beach. They looked so damn happy. But they were white. Probably lived somewhere nearby, in a real house, with a real family. They could afford this. All of it.

He hopped on the #3, got off on Crenshaw, caught the #5, and headed for PCH. Within ten minutes he was standing on the corner of PCH and Crenshaw with his thumb in the air, walking northwest, his back to the rising sun.

At around ten a.m. (he wasn't exactly sure about the time since he didn't own a watch) a VW van that looked like it had just slipped out of the 1970s slowed down and pulled up to the curb between a McDonald's and some New Age hole-in-the-wall called The Psychic Eye. Ernesto was surprised to see an older white man with graying hair sitting behind the wheel. Older men usually never stopped for Ernesto. They were too afraid of having their wallet ripped off or somethin'. Sure, Ernesto was a mugger, but he'd never rip off somebody who was doing him a favor. That'd just be wrong. Most white dudes were scared of Ernesto. It took him a long time to figure that out. At first he was offended. Then he tried to use it to his advantage. After all, if they're gonna be scared of you, you might as well give 'em good reason to be.

But *this* dude was different. He was slowin' down, and Ernesto was fuckin' glad about that. He'd walked an impossibly long stretch of PCH plenty of times before, and he wasn't in the mood to repeat that experience.

The dude was big and flabby. As if he'd played football many years ago, but now all that muscle had turned to mush. He wore a wine-red corduroy jacket over a black T-shirt, dark blue jeans, and flip-flip sandals. He had a wide, boyish smile that made him look much younger than he probably was. A full head of silver hair. He had to be in his fifties, at least. An old man.

An old man who stuck his arm out the window and said, "Say, kid, where're you going?"

"I'm headin' toward Venice Beach. Gotta meet someone there. You goin' in that direction?"

The man laughed. "Yeah, that general direction. I can probably drop you off pretty close. Hop in if you want. I might talk your ear off, though."

"Shit, I don't mind." Ernesto walked around the side of the van and climbed into the passenger seat.

"We can't go anywhere until you've got your seat belt on," the man said.

Ernesto strapped in. "I hate these things."

"So do I," the man said, putting his foot on the gas. They eased back into traffic. "I hate seat belts. I hate having to put my cigarette out in restaurants and bars. I hate paying taxes. I hate wearing a helmet when I ride a motorcycle. I hate getting a ticket for parking my car over eighteen inches from the curb. And I hate jay-walking tickets. But what the fuck're you gonna do? We live in America, don't we? It's hard to do what you want without offending somebody."

Ernesto laughed. "I know what you mean."

"My name's Harold," the man said. "What's yours?"

"Ernesto."

"You supposed to be in school right now?"

Ernesto waved his hand in the air. He leaned his head back against the vinyl seat and watched the scenery whiz by. Ernesto dreamed of the day he could have his own car, maybe even a van like this, and just *go* and not look back; he wanted to drive the entire length of PCH and see what was waiting for him on the other end of it. "Oh, I don't like school that much. I leave when I want to. I felt like goin' to the beach today. It's that kind of day. Who could sit in a classroom on a morning like this?"

He stuck his hand out the window, felt the wind blowing against his skin. The sky was bright blue, the sun so warm and bright.

Harold laughed—a bellowing, hearty kind of laugh. "Jesus, you could be me when I was a kid. I never liked to be indoors. And I never liked to be told what to do."

"Yeah?" Ernesto took a second look at the man. The jacket fit him real well, almost as if it was tailored for his lumpy body. He looked like an eccentric college professor. If Ernesto had seen him walking down the street, he's the kind of guy he and Julio would've mugged. He looked like money. *Easy* money.

"What do you do?" Ernesto said. "You know, for a living?"

"Nothing that would interest you. Real estate. Boring stuff. I'm semi-retired at this point. Sometimes I think I'd like to cut out entirely and go back to my hitchhiking days."

"*You* used to hitchhike?"

"When I was your age? Hell, I used to live on the road during the summers. I didn't have a car when I was fifteen, sixteen, so that's how me and my friends got around. In the summer of '68 I hitchhiked from Santa Cruz all the way to D.C. and back again. It wasn't a problem until the seventies when those slasher movies started comin' out. Then everybody got paranoid and afraid. It's too bad. I think something's lost in America when you can't get around by just stickin' your thumb in the air. Kids are too scared these days. Not adventurous at all. Take my kid. Tim's real serious, *all* the time. He moved out when he was eighteen. Got a job as a manager at Robinson's. Nice kid. Handsome, not like me at all." Harold laughed. "He's twenty and he's already married and has a kid. Little boy."

"Yeah? What's the kid's name?"

Harold furrowed his brow. "I really don't know. I've never met him."

"You've never met your grandson?"

"Yeah. It's like I was saying. Tim's just way too serious. Works all the time. Doesn't have a spare minute for his old man, not anymore. He spent his whole childhood just working and saving money. He never had any of the experiences I had when I was a kid, or like you're having now. Nose to the grindstone."

Ernesto laughed. "My mom would be happy if I was that way."

Harold nodded. "Of course, but sometimes it's just good to play. You can't learn everything you need to learn in a god damn classroom, that's for sure. All teachers are stupid. Keep that in mind."

Ernesto laughed again. "Why do you say that?"

"It's obvious. Just think about it. If they weren't stupid, they wouldn't be teaching, right? I mean, who would willingly deal with a bunch of brats all days for that amount of money if they could make a decent wage somewhere else? They're fuckups who failed in every aspect of their life, and now they want to dedicate their lives to spreading that failure like a virus among all their students. I never met a teacher who knew anything worthwhile. Everything I learned about business I learned on my own. Everything I have in this life—my house, my cars, my business, my family—I got by breaking the rules, not by following them. Keep that in mind too."

Ernesto was beginning to like this guy. He'd always suspected teachers were stupid, but he could never pinpoint the reason why. He just assumed *he* was stupid for even thinking such a thing. To meet a grownup who shared his views…well, it was another revelation.

"You're a pretty cool guy, man. Are you sure you're into real estate? You don't sell drugs or somethin'?"

The man laughed that bellowing laugh again. "Why? You got any?"

Ernesto shrugged. "I've got some bud on me. Want to buy some?"

"Sure, why not? How much you got?"

"Y'know, a bag…." He let the sentence trail off. He wasn't sure how much to charge this guy. Could he pull twenty-five bucks out of him?

"Sounds good to me," Harold said. "Is forty enough?"

"Are you serious? Yeah, man, that's fine."

"Damn, I haven't smoked pot in years. It's about time I got back into it. I know just where we can go. I'll even share it with you."

"Serious? Don't you have to be at work or something?"

"I have to be at work whenever I *say* I have to be at work. That's the beauty of being your own boss. Play your cards right, maybe you can go into business for yourself someday."

"That sounds sweet, man."

Ernesto leaned back in the seat and imagined what it would be like to not be bound by all the rules and regulations he'd grown up with. He'd watched his mother slowly turn haggard and wrinkled as the years crushed down on her…slowly, slowly. Not due to age, but because of worry and responsibility. Of always having to "do the right thing." Having to "toe the line." What the hell was the point? What was the point of living in a world where somebody like his mother could work herself to death trying to follow the rules every second of the day…where everybody was so busy trying to win that nobody ended up being anything but a loser in the end? Ernesto lived with losers every day. Losers on the bus. Losers standing behind the lecterns at school. Losers passing their bad habits down to him in the form of "good advice." He existed in a neighborhood of losers. A city of losers. And it was all designed that way. By the people who made the rules.

Fat white men with a lot of free time on their hands.

And apparently the people who made the rules could break them.

That had never occurred to Ernesto before. Whenever he broke the law, he always felt vaguely guilty. After all, he was *breaking the rules*. What would his mother say? But his mother was hypnotized like all the rest.

This man beside him had become successful by doing only what he wanted. And that's the life Ernesto had always dreamed of, even if he was never fully aware of it until just now.

Harold followed PCH up a ways, then turned off onto a road that led up into the hills of Malaga Cove. Ernesto had been up here once before during one of his many solitary jaunts. It was a beautiful place, far more beautiful than anything he'd ever seen growing up in Wilmington, except maybe exotic places on TV. The cliffs of Malaga Cove overlooked sheer drops that led straight down into the crashing, white tides of the blue Pacific. The whole scene looked like another world, like something out of *The Lord of the Rings* movies, some dreamlike, computer-generated fantasyland that had always been inaccessible to him.

The houses perched on the cliffs high above him seemed so precarious. How much did those houses cost? What if an earthquake hit? Weren't the people inside them scared of falling into the sea? Weren't any of them afraid to die?

Harold turned down a narrow side road surrounded by large trees and gnarled bushes. He switched off the engine. Just past the trees, you could hear the sound of seagulls cawing at one another over the swelling waves. And behind him, the sound of an occasional car driving past on its way up to the very top of the cliffs.

Harold said, "Let's see the merchandise, my friend."

Ernesto pulled out the ziplock bag and opened it.

Harold's nostrils flared. He closed his eyes and allowed the aroma to waft into his gaping nostrils. "Ahhh…I haven't smelled something as good as that in such a long time. Do you have a pipe?"

"Shit, I don't leave home without it." Ernesto reached into his pocket and whipped out a red, green, and white pipe decorated with the patterns of the Mexican flag. It was still clogged with brownish resin. "I don't mean to be rude, man, but I need to see some cash first."

"Oh, of course…of course." Harold pulled out a brown leather wallet from his back pocket and reached inside for the cash. He gave him twice what he promised.

Ernesto was shocked. "Are you sure you're not makin' some mistake?" he said. Normally he would've just pocketed the money without saying a word, but somehow he didn't feel like taking advantage of this strange man.

"Keep it," Harold said, taking both the pipe and the ziplock bag from Ernesto. "Buy a nice dinner for yourself. I really appreciate you givin' an old guy like me a break from all the nonsense."

"What do you mean? What kind of nonsense?"

Harold waved his hand in the air. "Responsibilities." Harold packed the pipe like a chronic smoker. He whipped out a lighter from the glove compartment and lit up. He took in a lung full of smoke, held it for awhile, then let it all out. The smoke filled the van. A big smile crept across Harold's wrinkled face. "This is as good as it gets."

"Yeah?" Ernesto laughed. "Well, I'm glad I could help you out."

Harold passed him the pipe. Ernesto took a huge drag. He'd already made way more money than he would have if he'd gone on to Venice. He couldn't wait to get back home and buy something for Margarita. Somewhere behind him, seagulls cried out to each other in their secret language. The air smelled so good up here. So salty and fresh….

Ernesto passed the pipe back to Harold.

"I used to take Tim up here," Harold said in between drags. "I'd like to do that again someday. All three of us, him and his son. I think they'd enjoy it up here, don't you?"

"Sure," Ernesto said. "You could have a picnic, get stoned. Why not?" Ernesto burst out laughing.

Harold just stared at him for a second, with no emotion at all, before finally joining in. Now they were giggling together. He passed the pipe back to Ernesto.

"You seem like a cool dad to me," Ernesto said, taking another long drag. "Any dad who doesn't bogart the pipe is a good dad. Fuck, let's put that on a coffee mug. We could sell it."

Harold giggled. "Yes…a novelty item for Father's Day. It'd sell like…like…fuck, it'd sell like…marijuana, I guess. I don't know."

Now Ernesto was giggling too. "I wish you were my dad."

"Really?"

"Fuck, yeah. You kiddin'? Even Julio would be jealous of me if I had you as a dad, and his dad lets him drink beer. I always thought that was so cool. Not as cool as this."

Harold reached out and put his hand on Ernesto's knee. He started patting it. "I'm having a real good time." His massive hand slid up Ernesto's jeans and grabbed a hold of his crotch. It happened so fast, at first Ernesto didn't think it was really happening. He thought he was imagining it.

"What're you doin'?" Ernesto said.

"Let's get in the back of the van now," Harold said. Through the blue denim jeans, he started rubbing Ernesto's penis with swift, circular motions.

Ernesto yanked his leg away from Harold's beefy fingers. He grabbed for the handle on the door, dropping the pipe on the floor. He realized he still had his seatbelt on.

"Don't freak out," Harold said calmly, grabbing for him again. "It's okay… I've got more money… You want more money, is that it?"

"Son of a bitch!" Ernesto ceasing fiddling with the seatbelt long enough to haul off and plant his fist into Harold's pudgy face. He heard cartilage shatter as a stream of blood spurted onto Ernesto's jacket.

Harold screeched like a little girl as his eyes flared with anger and betrayal. One pupil even seemed to grow larger than the other as he lunged at Ernesto. He started clawing at Ernesto's face with his yellowing fingernails.

Ernesto managed to hit the button that released the seatbelt, then backed up against the passenger door, lifted up his legs, and slammed his dirt-covered Nike tennis shoes into Harold's solar plexus. Air escaped Harold's lungs. He gasped. He was trying to say something but couldn't form words.

Ernesto opened the passenger door and tumbled out of the van. His palms impacted hard with the pebble-speckled sand. The impact stung, but Ernesto ignored the sensation and scrambled to his feet, dashed towards the narrow road they had taken to get up here. Behind him he heard Harold yell, "*Stop!*" He kept on running…until he heard the gunshot and saw the bullet take out a huge chunk of the tree only two feet from his head.

Ernesto ceased his flight, remained motionless. He turned around.

Harold stood near the bumper, waving a .38 revolver at his chest. "I…was trying…to be *nice*. Get back over here." Harold swung open the double doors that led into the back of the van.

Somewhere deep inside his stomach, Ernesto began shaking. Until this second, he hadn't had time to think. Just act. Fight back. Run. He'd seen things like this happen in movies, but it could never happen to him. He could tell who was crazy and who wasn't. He could tell. It was easy.

He had an instinct for such things.

Harold waved his gun at the back of the van. "Don't make me say it again, friend." Harold was glancing from side to side, as if afraid somebody might show up at any moment.

Ernesto stared at the back of the van. He was going to be murdered.

Get him to shoot you. Run. Run now while you still can. Better to be dead than….

But he didn't run. He didn't want to die. So he walked slowly toward the van. When he was within reach, Harold reached out swiftly, grabbed him by the shoulder, and pushed him inside, the barrel of the gun pressed into his ribs.

"Sit down," Harold said.

Ernesto sat.

The back of the van had carpeting on the floor and pleasant looking posters on the walls. Very tasteful. They looked like classical paintings, like the kind of thing you saw hanging in the counselor's office at school. Or that museum in L.A., the one he'd gone to once on a field trip in the fifth grade.

Harold pressed the gun against Ernesto's forehead and told him to get down on his knees.

"Please don't," Ernesto whispered. His voice was quivering.

"Do as I *say*!"

Ernesto got down on his knees. With one hand, Harold undid his belt and let his pants drop to the floor. His penis was huge and erect and so swollen it almost appeared purple.

"C'mon, you know what to do," Harold said, pressing the barrel of the gun against Ernesto's left temple. "Don't pretend like you've never done it before. Why else would you be out hitchhiking on the side of the road? I'm not falling for the innocent routine. Neither will anyone else."

Anybody else? Who else will ever know? I'm not getting out of here. I'm not getting out of here alive.

He said nothing. Shut off his brain. Swung his left arm upwards in a swift arc, knocking Harold's arm away from him. Harold reflexively pulled the trigger. A bullet burrowed first through the carpet, then the metal floor beneath. Ernesto lunged, ramming the top of his head into

Harold's crotch. Harold lost his balance, getting caught up in the Levis pooled around his ankles, and tumbled backwards. Ernesto leaped on top of him, grabbing Harold's right wrist with both hands. The moment Harold's ass slammed against the floor, the fleeting millisecond in which his grip loosened ever so slightly, Ernesto ripped the revolver out of his fist. Ernesto scooted backwards across the carpet, his ass never leaving the floor, sweat pouring down his forehead, his heart beating against his ribcage, wrapping his fingers around the hilt of the gun.

Harold screamed like a child throwing a temper tantrum: "Give that back to me, it's *mine!*" Harold lunged, his pants still around his ankles, his fingers reaching for Ernesto's eyes.

Ernesto shut his eyes tight and pulled the trigger. An explosion tore through his hands. His wrists snapped backwards. Then silence.

Slowly, Ernesto opened his eyes. Saw Harold lying flat on his back, the top of his head spilt open like a seedless watermelon. Smelled the metallic gun smoke burning his nostrils. Felt the warm blood and pieces of stringy flesh clinging to his face, his neck, his arms, and the back of his hands. The churro rising in his throat. He wanted to retch. Calm down… calm down….

He closed his eyes again, lowered his arms, allowed the gun—still clutched in his hands—to rest on the carpet.

He wanted to go back now. Back home. Hide in his room. Play video games. Talk with Margarita on the phone. Bullshit with Julio in the parking lot of Vons. Avoid doing homework. Dream of a life without responsibilities. He wanted to go back.

But when he opened his eyes again, the body was still there. Nothing had changed.

Ernesto climbed over the corpse and out of the van, shut the doors behind him, walked around to the driver's seat, slid behind the wheel. He set the gun down on the dashboard.

He sat there for a moment, smelled the familiar scent of marijuana in the air. He glanced down and saw the pipe lying there. I better hide this, he thought. I don't want to get arrested.

He climbed out of the driver's seat, returned to the back of the van, and slipped the pipe between a couple of cardboard boxes beside the motionless body. He felt relieved he had solved that problem.

He stared at the body for a while, taking in all the details, before reality began to fall into place. He knelt down beside the corpse and pulled out the leather wallet he'd seen earlier. There was five hundred and thirty dollars waiting inside. He slipped the cash in his pocket, then rummaged through the various cards tucked away inside a tiny plastic window. The name on the ID said Jacob Bilmes. (Harold wasn't even his real name.) He lived in Manhattan Beach just off Pacific Avenue. Ernesto had strolled through that area with Julio late one night. Pretty nice area. Good for muggings. But they hadn't mugged anybody that night. A cop car strolled along beside them slowly, menacingly, and the cop stuck his head out the window and asked them what they were doing. Neither of them had a good answer. The cop hassled them for thirty minutes before ordering them to go home. But apparently the cop should've been more concerned about the freaks who *lived* there.

Ernesto rummaged through the other cards: several platinum cards, proof of membership in the Elks, a debit card, proof of membership in the Shriners, a social security card, proof of membership in the Scottish Rite, a Vons club card, proof of membership in the PTA, a business card for a criminal defense attorney in Huntington Beach (Ernesto smiled—should he give the dude a call?), proof of membership in the American Hunter's Club, a faded color photograph of a small boy (his son?), and a more recent photo of an older blond woman with a '80s hairstyle, her skinny arm around Harold/Jacob at some kind of festive get together. Other partiers, old men, were milling around in the background. They were all dressed up for the occasion. Jacob was wearing a funny hat on his head and an ornate apron. Everybody was smiling.

At the bottom of the stack was one other card. For some reason it caught Ernesto's eye. A business card. Bold black lettering against eggshell white:

TIMOTHY BILMES, MANAGER
ROBINSON'S
DEL AMO MALL

And beneath that was an exact address and phone number. Timothy. That's gotta be the son. The one who doesn't…talk to him…anymore.

Ernesto glanced again at the fading photograph, the one with the smiling boy in it, and tears began to form in his eyes. He tried to blink them away but couldn't. He collapsed onto his butt and started heaving sobs into his hand.

Until at last, without really even thinking about it, he took the photograph of the child and the business card and slipped them into his back pocket. The other cards he sprinkled on Jacob's dead body.

He slid behind the steering wheel again. Beside the driver's seat was a plastic drink holder; inside sat a warm, unopened bottle of Aquafina water. Ernesto grabbed it, snapped off the plastic cap, and slowly poured the water over his face and jacket, trying to wash the mess away.

He started up the van. He tore out of there, dirt flying behind the wheels, as he raced down the narrow sloping path that would take him back into civilization, or at least the civilization he knew. He never wanted to see the ocean again. Certainly not Malaga Cove.

He left the seagulls and the salty air and the crashing ocean waves far behind him. He swung onto PCH and headed south, back toward Wilmington. He couldn't go straight home. His nerves were shot. He was still shaking a little. He had to tell somebody what happened. Not his mom. Not his brother. Not his girlfriend.

Julio. Julio would be the one to tell. They had shared so many crimes together. Why not this one as well?

He stared at the gun on the dashboard. So much can change in a few seconds. He grabbed the gun and slipped it beneath the driver's seat.

At around 12:30 Ernesto parked the van in a trash-ridden alley, about a block away from Julio's house. Julio always came home for lunch, if he could manage to leap the gate and get past all the narcs who patrolled the campus. That was never much of a problem. The people they hired to patrol the campus were ex-hoodlums themselves. They didn't care about anything except an easy paycheck.

(Not that there was anything wrong with an easy paycheck.)

Ernesto leaped up onto Julio's front porch. It was comforting to be back in his own environment. To see those familiar bars on the windows, the black iron screen door, the peeling white paint on the front door. Ernesto knocked on the door, the metal rattling like a giant bird cage.

Julio answered the door. Cartoons were on in the background. Julio loved cartoons. SpongeBob was a favorite.

"Fuck, where were you today?" Julio said. "Margarita's lookin' for you. Said she wanted to talk to you real bad. She told me to tell you to call her right away." Julio's place always smelled like dog shit. They kept five huge dogs, never letting them leave, in a space that was far too small for them.

"She can wait. I've got somethin' real important to show you."

"Man, you ain't lyin'. It must be somethin' fuckin' *huge* if you ain't pussywhipped by that bitch no more."

"Yeah, I guess you could say it's pretty huge. C'mon."

"Right now? But I was just about to put a hotdog in the microwave. You want one?"

"This is *waaay* more important." Julio didn't look convinced. "Trust me, okay?"

Julio sighed and rolled his eyes. "All right. Where're we going?"

"Just around the corner." Ernesto led him away from the porch, past a group of little kids walking home from school. Either the school let them out early or they were ditching. They were all laughing and smiling. No worries in the world. No responsibilities. Not yet.

When the kids were out of sight, Ernesto pulled Julio into the alley. "It's right here."

"Whose van is this?" Julio said.

"Mine."

"What're you talking about? You *stole* this?"

"No...not exactly. I...I shot this dude. Right through the head."

Julio laughed nervously. "Oh, I get it. Why bother mugging people when you can go all the way, right? Shit, man. I'm missin' my favorite show."

"You don't believe me?"

"No."

"I'll show you then."

Julio seemed worried, and a little scared. It was kind of fun, just for a few seconds, to have Julio lookin' at him like some badass motherfucker in a movie. The hero who shoots first and asks questions later. The star who can get the job done and nobody fucks over. Ever. The guy whose only responsibility is to fuck shit up and then leave town, lookin' for trouble somewhere else. No worries at all, till the sequel.

He could tell Julio the whole truth later on.

Ernesto glanced from side to side, to see if anybody was coming, then swung open the doors. He gestured toward the shadowy, gaping maw that led into the back of the van. For a moment, he felt like a painter unveiling a new piece of work. He felt proud.

Julio stared. Julio took two steps toward the van, put his foot up on the silver fender, leaned into the warm darkness. He reached out and touched the bloody shoulder of the fat man. It did not move. His fingertip came away covered in moist redness.

Julio stared at his fingertip, his face went white...then collapsed onto his knees and puked all over the pavement. The vile brownish mess went everywhere, splattering on Julio's pant legs.

"Oh shit, you all right?" Ernesto said, slamming the doors shut.

Julio was staring at him so strangely.

The look on Julio's face, the sight of his best friend gagging on his knees, jolted Ernesto out of his fleeting moment of pride. He whispered,

"I *had* to do it. I had no choice."

"You tried to mug him?"

"No," Ernesto said. "He tried to kill me. He wanted me…he wanted me to do shit to him, man. Weird stuff. Gay shit. So I took the gun from him and shot the fucker. I *shot* him."

Julio's eyes were widening even further. "What kinda gay shit? What do you mean?"

"He wanted me to suck him off, man. So I said…I said, 'Fuck you, faggot!' and I grabbed the gun out of his hand and shot him through the fuckin' skull, man. Fuck you. Fuck you, you son of a bitch!" Ernesto was now yelling at the closed doors.

Julio was growing paler by the second.

Ernesto leaned down, helped Julio to his feet. "I think I better get you back home. You look worse than he does."

"I'm okay," Julio said. "Really. I just… I want to know…more about…."

"I'll tell you the whole story later."

"What're you gonna do with *him*?"

"Leave him somewhere."

"Where?"

"I dunno. Somewhere far away."

Julio nodded. "Maybe…maybe you're right. I need to go back home."

"I might need your help later on. Remember, you can't tell *anybody* about this," Ernesto said. "You *got* that, Julio?" His voice became deep and intimidating. It was as if he were trying to be a tough guy, like some actor he'd seen in a film.

Julio shrank away from him, adopting the only role left. "I know," he said, a little bit timorously. "I know. If…if I see Margarita again, what should I…?"

"Tell her I'm busy."

"All right. Call me if you need me, man… Y'know, I'll be there."

Ernesto nodded silently and watched him stagger down the alley.

Ernesto said nothing. He knew he wouldn't ask him for any more help. He just got back into the van.

He drove away.

Ernesto had no idea where he was headed. He cruised around, not thinking about anything except the glare of the sun on the shiny black concrete and all the cars in front of him. He must've blanked out for a while, because the next thing he knew he was in Manhattan Beach. Headed for Jacob's neighborhood. His exact address. Why? What would be the point of that?

He thought about leaving the van behind a Safeway after dark. But he knew that was a stupid idea. It would be found by morning. There was nothing to connect him to the murder, he was sure of that, but he'd rather not worry about it at all for a while. Better to leave it somewhere far away. Very far away.

I'll take it back to Malaga Cove, he thought. Right where it happened. People camp out there all the time. Nobody would check on it for a while.

He stared at his reflection in the rearview mirror. Puzzled by what he saw. Who was this panicked, insane creature? The reflection asked him, But what about the gun?

I'll drop it off a cliff...right into the ocean.

You better wipe the prints off it first. Just in case. It could wash up on shore.

Ernesto nodded. Good thinking. I'm glad you're here.

So am I. Man, it's like being the star of your own gangsta movie.

Ernesto started laughing. Was any of this really happening?

He decided to head west toward Palos Verdes Blvd. He knew that would take him to the general vicinity of the Cove. He wanted this over and done with *now*. He wanted to start the day all over again. Wanted to go back to sleep and wake up and call Margarita and—

And what?

His stomach, his head, the space right behind his eyes, all felt so empty.

On North Sepulveda Blvd. he noticed the cop car cruising behind him. Started to get worried. Started to speed up.

Calm the fuck down, his reflection said. You're just drawin' attention to yourself, man.

The siren went off.

Oh, shit.

Julio? Did Julio...?

As Ernesto stepped on the gas he felt it all slipping away. The nothingness behind his eyes melted to be replaced by *something*: a genuine feeling. A sensation. An emotion. An overwhelming desire to live. To be free.

A desire he suddenly realized had been there lodged inside his gut forever, motivating his entire life. Without ever knowing it.

But not now. Now he knew *exactly* why he sped up to fifty, cutting through a red light and almost getting hit by a huge green China Shipping truck. The truck shrieked as it skidded to an abrupt stop in the middle of a crosswalk, barely missing Ernesto's side of the van by inches. The truck blocked the cop's pursuit.

Fuck Palos Verdes. They'd never let him get anywhere near it now. Ernesto turned left onto Manhattan Beach Blvd. and almost hit a group of retarded kids shambling through a crosswalk. School books went flying into the air and landed in a scattered pile on the concrete. Ernesto reached underneath the seat, put the revolver on the dashboard, where he could get at it quickly if he needed to, then stepped on the gas. He cranked up to fifty-five. He glanced at the clock in the dash. Almost 3:30.

In the rearview mirror he saw the cop car peel around the corner, sirens blaring and flashing, trying to cover the distance that now separated them. Ernesto breathed a sigh of relief when he reached Inglewood Blvd. Smooth, perfect sidewalks gave way to cracked concrete lined with unhealthy, leafless trees. He slammed the gas even harder. Two miles whizzed by. He sped onto the 405, not really sure where he was headed, but knowing he refused to end up like the fat mound of bloody flesh in the back.

* * * *

And south…first on the 405 for a quick jaunt, a flotilla of cop cars and helicopters attached to his ass, then back to the surface streets, Crenshaw Blvd., then Torrance Blvd., then west toward the Mall.

When he was a kid, watching live police chases on the TV, he always wondered what *he* would do in that situation. How do you get away from a bunch of cops and a fuckin' rovin' eye in the sky? How?

One time he asked his dad that very question. And his dad said, "You get lost somewhere. In an enclosed area. In a group of people. Blend in with crowd. Be calm. Act normal. *Know* you're not guilty."

Know you're not guilty.

How did his dad know that?

Where the fuck are you right now?

Ernesto knew exactly where he was headed. How many times had he taken the #3 down to Del Amo Mall? A billion times since he was ten?

He swerved into the massive parking lot outside the main entrance to the Mall, barely avoiding pedestrians and other cars. He screeched to a halt on the sidewalk, leaped out of the car, not even looking behind him to check out the horde of cop cars that were right behind him. The helicopter couldn't help but lose sight of him the second he entered the building.

To his right, a Carl's Jr.; to his left, an entrance to the bathrooms and the twisting gray corridors that ran behind the Mall. They were built for the employees, for janitors. Ernesto had played in those corridors since he was five years old when he'd break away from his parents and wander around through the bowels of the Mall, pretending he was lost in a labyrinth filled with monsters.

And now he was. He ran down the corridor, taking off his black jacket as he did so, then ducked into the men's bathroom for a single second and dropped the jacket in a trash can. Into the corridor again. Nobody was there. So he ran at full speed, curving around and around, all the way to another entrance that opened out into a separate area of the Mall. He reached the double doors, stood still for a few seconds, trying to calm his breathing, combed his hair with his fingers, wiped sweat from his brow, then opened the doors and wandered into the massive throng of Mall shoppers. Just another consumer out for a pleasant afternoon. Another high school kid haunting the Mall right after school.

Nobody paid any attention to him. He walked over to a lemonade stand, pulled out Jacob's money, and purchased a nice tall cup of lemonade filled with crushed ice. This was the best lemonade in the world. He'd thought so ever since he was a kid.

He strolled over to a block of concrete decorated with ornate blue tiles and sat near a group of teenagers who could easily have been his friends from school. He sat there, sipping on the drink, listening to their mundane conversation ("I don't understand. How come Steve doesn't call me anymore?" "Girl, the second you sleep with a guy, forget it. They're gone. You can't just give it away. Make 'im wait.") and watched in confusion with everyone else as a bunch of cops poured into the Mall like a swarm of worker bees in search of honey. ("You in trouble, girl. They after yo ass." "Yeah? I think they gonna arrest *you* fo' that shit you wearin'.") And all the teenage girls were abuzz now and laughing and giggling and Ernesto struck up a conversation with one of them and made a joke about the cops and laughed along with them. He talked to her for about ten minutes, got her phone number, then wandered off, the cup of lemonade still in his hand.

Walked all the way to the entrance of Robinson's. Threw the cup of lemonade in the trash can outside, entered. A woman dressed like a runway model tried to squirt him with cologne. He said no thank you and kept walking. The muzak was gentle and annoying at the same time. He wished it would stop. Funny, he'd never even noticed the music all those times before.

He walked up to one of the cashiers. A pretty blonde, about his age, dressed very smartly. Adult and sexy. According to her tag, her name was Ashley. She was way out of Ernesto's league. "Excuse me," he said, "I'd...like to speak to the manager. Please. Mr. Timothy Bilmes?"

"A problem?"

"No...not with the store." He glanced at his surroundings, trying to appear casual. "I guess you could say it's kind of...a family emergency. Tim should know about it right away. Someone should let 'im know."

Ashley nodded, then got on the mike to call the manager to register 2.

"Thank you," Ernesto said.

The man who approached the register a few seconds later was tall and lanky. Brown hair cut short and stylish. He was wearing a dark dress shirt with slacks and a tie. He was only a few years older than Ernesto, but he looked like a real adult. His name tag identified him as TIM, MANAGER.

"This...*gentleman*," Ashley said, "asked for you. He claims it's a family emergency."

Tim looked confused and a little scared. "Family emergency? What do you mean?"

He has a two-year-old kid at home, Ernesto thought. He's thinking about his little boy.

"I...don't we should talk about it here," Ernesto said. "Can we go outside? By the fountain?"

Tim seemed reluctant, but he followed Ernesto outside Robinson's to the enclosed courtyard. In the center sat the fountain. The water erupted from the top of a half-sphere made of tiny glass squares. You could reach out and feel the water pouring down the curved surface of the sphere. Ernesto did that now as he sat down. Nobody else was sitting near them.

"What's all this about?" Tim said, refusing to sit. He seemed impatient.

"Please...sit down," Ernesto said.

"Why?"

"I know why you don't want your father anywhere around your son."

Tim lowered, slowly. He looked a little shocked. He sat beside him. "How...could you know that?"

"I met your dad today. I was hitchhiking down PCH around ten o'clock and he picked me up. He told me his name was Harold. He bought some marijuana from me. Then he drove me to the top of Malaga Cove and put a gun to my head and tried to make me do shit to him I didn't want to do."

Tim shut his eyes.

"He told me about you. And how you don't want him to see your son. And I think I know why. But you don't have to worry about him anymore 'cause I took the gun from him and shot him. I took these off his body."

He reached into his back pocket and pulled out the photograph of Tim as a child along with Tim's frayed business card. The manager of Robinson's took both items from him. He stared at the photograph for a very long time.

"I didn't want to kill him," Ernesto said. He felt tears beginning to form in his eyes. "I never wanted to kill nobody. I feel all cold inside now and I don't know if that feelin's ever gonna go away. I feel dead inside and part of me wants to die like him but another part of me wants to live... I want to live so I can show that son of a bitch he can't destroy me. Y'know what I mean?"

Tim nodded slowly. Tears began to form in his eyes too.

"He told me they wouldn't listen to me. And he's right. They're not gonna believe me. Just look at me. They're not gonna believe me. Unless you tell them. Tell them all what kind of a man he really was."

Tim stared down at the ground. He shook his head back and forth. "I can't."

"*Why?*"

Tim's tears had gone away. "I can't do that to my family. I can't... talk about it."

"So what am *I* supposed to do?"

Tim couldn't look at him. He just kept staring at the photograph.

"They're looking for me," Ernesto said. "Right now. I'm not getting out of here unless you help me."

Tim remained silent for a moment. A very long moment. Then stuffed the photograph and the card in his pocket and stood up. "Wait here."

Ernesto shot to his feet. He grabbed Tim by the sleeve. His palm was still wet from the fountain. "Are you turnin' me in?"

"No. I'll be back. I *will*."

Somehow, the wounded dead stare in his eyes didn't look like that of a liar. Ernesto sat down. He had an instinct for such things. Tim left.

Ernesto sat staring at the fountain, all the nice little moments coming back to him, all the pleasant memories of window shopping with his mom in the Mall. Always so nice to get out of the house, out of the neighborhood, away from Dad.

Where are you right now?

Tim returned within a few minutes. "I told them I had a family emergency to tend to. I've never even called in sick before, so it shouldn't be a problem."

Tim headed for the huge glass double doors only a few feet away that led out into the open air to the second floor of a multilevel parking structure. Tim's black Honda CRX sat waiting for them in Area H. Tim slid behind the steering wheel and told Ernesto to get in.

"Where the hell're we going?" Ernesto said.

"Away from here," Tim said. He reached into the back seat and grabbed an expensive pair of blue jeans and a black sweat shirt, then threw them at Ernesto. "Put these on."

"Will they fit?"

"Well enough to hide you. You look like you're used to wearing baggy clothes. It shouldn't be too much of a problem."

Ernesto made the change in silence while Tim dug around in the back seat for more clothes. "Here's a baseball cap," he said, "and a pullover sweater. I don't need them anymore. Just take them with you."

"Where?"

"Where do you want to go?"

"Not to jail."

Tim nodded. "*Where?*"

"What happens if they catch me?"

Tim said without hesitation, "I'll lie. I'll say I don't know what you're talking about. I'll sit on the stand and swear to God and anybody else who'll listen that my dad was an upstanding guy, the best of the best. He would never be capable of doing something as horrible as that. And I couldn't be where I am today without him. That…that, at least, is true."

"But *why?*"

Tim's hands tightened on the steering wheel. "I won't talk about it. I *won't.*"

Silence descended on them once again. At last Ernesto said, "Take me to the Greyhound bus station, the one in Long Beach. That's the closest."

"Where're you going from there?"

"You need to know?"

Tim shook his head. "No, I don't."

They left the parking structure and through the police barricade with no problem. *Nobody suspicious in here, officer. Nobody at all.* Checking himself out in the rearview mirror, Ernesto almost thought he could pass for a white man when he was dressed like this.

A comforting thought.

Via the freeway it took about a half hour to get from Torrance to the Long Beach Greyhound Station. Ernesto sat in silence staring at the scenery whiz past. He had just passed it in the opposite direction with a city full of cops on his ass. It was strange seeing it now, only an hour later, with nothing pursuing him but his past. Memories of Wilmington.

He realized now how much he hated that place. How much he had always wanted to leave it behind.

Tim started talking. About his son. His wife. How much he loved both of them. He was working as a manager at Robinson's while also going to college part-time at UCLA. He was majoring in International Relations, but he didn't bother to explain what that meant. And Ernesto didn't bother to ask.

He had met Patricia, his wife, in a political science class during a summer session at UCLA. She was from a rich family in Bel Air. A very, *very* rich family. They were influential in local politics. Her father looked down on Tim the second he saw him, and still did to this day. He considered him to be nothing more than "surf trash" from Manhattan Beach. But Tim was determined to prove him wrong. He was not tainted. He was *not* trash. He could be somebody. He was going to go into politics someday. And then Patricia's father would see. And he'd know. Everybody would.

"Why the fuck do I care about all this?" Ernesto said.

"Because. I need you to understand. I don't like lying. I don't *want* to lie."

"Who's asking you to?"

"If you don't get caught, then you won't put me in a position of having to lie."

Ernesto laughed bitterly. "Don't worry. I won't get caught."

Tim nodded. He seemed to be relieved.

"I want you to understand somethin' too," Ernesto said. "I didn't like killing him. I never want to do something like that again."

"Well...I should've done it a long time ago."

"I guess I did your dirty work for you."

Tim did not respond. Before he knew it, they were pulling into the parking lot of the Greyhound Station. Ernesto grabbed a plastic Robinson's bag from the floor and stuffed his clothes in them, his real ones.

His luggage.

Tim did not turn off the engine. He reached into his wallet and pulled out two fifty-dollar bills. "This is all I have on me, I swear. I'd give you more if I could."

"That'll do," Ernesto said, grabbing the bills out of his hand. Combined with Jacob's cash, that would last him just long enough. "I hope you get what you want. I hope Pops gives you some respect. When he does, maybe I'll look you up again."

"Listen," Tim said, "I don't ever want to see your face again."

"That's funny," Ernesto said. "'Cause I never want to see your face again either. But I think I *will*. Maybe on the TV when you're all powerful and famous. Mr. Senator Man. That have a nice ring to it?"

Tim's brows narrowed to a point. "Are you fucking threatening me? I'm doing you a *favor*. I don't have any problem turning you in. Whether it's today or tomorrow, no one's gonna believe you. Don't ever forget that."

"No one's ever gonna let me forget it."

He slammed the door shut and walked slowly toward the entrance to the station. He heard Tim pulling out of the parking lot behind him. Going back home. To the wife and kids. To a future filled with hope. And responsibility.

Ernesto stood in the middle of the station staring at a giant map on the wall. So many places to go. Only one ticket to buy.

He closed his eyes and allowed his finger to fall where it might.

Seattle. He'd always heard great things about Seattle. The music scene. The pot. And it was so close to Canada. Why not?

He bought the first ticket for Washington. The bus was leaving at 6:00 p.m., only ten minutes from now.

He sat outside, right in front of the bus, waiting for the doors to open. When he finally got on board, he picked a seat near the back. Just like he'd done earlier this morning.

He settled back and watched the concrete gray Long Beach scenery drift away. As he closed his eyes, he remembered fucking Margarita last night. Around midnight. In the back of that beat-up car. He remembered her clawing at his back with her red lacquered nails as she uttered little squealing noises. He tried, tried so hard, to pull out right when he felt himself coming. But she refused to let him go, held him tightly in place between her long smooth legs a little too long. Almost as if she were doing it on purpose. Now, as calm silence descended upon his tired mind, he recalled those few drops of sperm that squirted out of him right before he wrenched himself away and ejaculated on her flat, toned midriff. He spread the mess around with his palm, feeling the muscles in her stomach. All that time on drill team had given her a perfect body. A body he was leaving behind along with everything else.

Along with whatever he might have left inside her.

He was losing his school, his mom, his brother, his friends, his future. Losing. Losing everything.

So why, as he drifted off to sleep, did he feel like a winner at last?

The grating sound of a bus merging onto a clogged freeway, an angry horn blaring three times in a row, leaked into his dream and transformed into the warning cry of an immense seagull circling over a shore of beached skeletons, humans, all of them lying face-down in dry desert-like sand, a familiar desolation, a faded snapshot now dwindling into the sundrenched distance.

✗

Robert Guffey's most recent book is *Bela Lugosi and the Monogram Nine*, coauthored with Gary D. Rhodes. Forthcoming is *Widow of the Amputation and Other Weird Crimes*, and his previous books include *Until the Last Dog Dies*, *Chameleon: A Strange but True Story of Invisible Spies, Heroin Addiction, and Homeland Security* and *Spies & Saucers*. He's also published short stories in such publications as *The Mailer Review*, *Phantom Drift*, *Postscripts*, and *Rosebud*.

BLEST BE THE TIE THAT BINDS
MICHAEL BRACKEN

Heather and Robert Connelly held their wedding reception on the expanse of lawn between the Union Revival Baptist Church and the two-story parsonage at the far end of the block. Because Robert could not conduct his own wedding ceremony, his best friend from seminary flew in from Pasadena to do the honors, and the entire congregation turned out to see their spiritual leader betrothed, filling the celebration center beyond official capacity. The lawn was awash with parishioners sporting their Sunday best when the bride and groom finally exited the church following the obligatory post-ceremony photographs, and they applauded when the heavy wooden doors opened, and the newly married couple descended the broad stone steps to join them.

The groom wore a fitted black suit over a white shirt and royal blue tie. Though purchased specifically for the wedding, their finances were such that the suit would soon be seeing duty at the many funerals over which Robert would preside as the pastor of a church with an aging congregation. His new wife was resplendent in a white, floor-length, fitted cap-sleeve gown covered in lace, a dress that would likely never be seen again once it returned from the dry cleaners. Her ash blond hair was swept up into a chignon and held in place with her grandmother's pearl-encrusted comb.

There had been no need to hire a caterer, for the Women's Auxiliary had smothered a long row of folding tables with food prepared in the church's kitchen or brought from their homes. Only the wedding cake, which was nowhere near large enough to serve all the guests, had been professionally prepared, and a variety of home-baked cakes covered the table next to it.

The gift table was equally burdened to overflowing, with several wrapped boxes relegated to the lawn beneath the table, and the gaily-wrapped shoebox with the slit in the top proved too small for the number of cards that guests tried to stuff into it.

Heather and Robert were first through the buffet line, and they took their places at the head table, unable to eat as parishioner after parishioner stopped to express best wishes. Once everyone had been served, the best man lifted a glass of sparkling grape juice and toasted the newlyweds, wishing them a long and fruitful life. Later, they cut the wedding cake and posed for the photographer. Then, together and separately, they tried to talk to every one of their guests. When his throat became parched, Robert refilled his glass of sparkling grape juice and was taking a sip when someone behind him spoke softly into his ear.

"You have such a beautiful bride," said the deep male voice. "It would be a shame if anything ever happened to her."

Robert stiffened and turned, too late to see the face of the man who had just spoken. He only saw the back of a dark-haired man in a blue suit walking toward the church parking lot. As Robert started after the man, the church treasurer stopped him. Before Harvey Johnson could speak, Robert asked, "Who was that—the man who was just talking to me?"

"I wasn't paying attention."

By then the dark-haired man in the blue suit had disappeared, Harvey was congratulating him on his marriage, and Heather was on his other side telling him it was time to start their honeymoon. As everyone showered them with birdseed, Heather and Robert ducked into the back of a waiting limousine for the ride to her parents' home, where they changed into comfortable clothing and then drove to a bed and breakfast several hours from home.

They would spend their wedding night in one of six private cabins and, for the first time since accepting the pastorship a year earlier following the unexpected death of his predecessor, Robert would not arise early the next morning to deliver Sunday service. His friend from seminary would perform those honors.

Though Robert had remained celibate since his first day at seminary, he lost his virginity at Bible camp when he was sixteen. So, he knew what to expect on his wedding night, but he did not truly appreciate his new wife's beauty until Heather walked out of the bathroom wearing nothing but a sheer white negligee and a shy smile. Though the stranger's comments at the reception weighed heavily on his mind during the drive to their honeymoon cabin, those thoughts, and every other thought, disappeared from Robert's mind as he took Heather into his arms and they consummated their marriage.

* * * *

The following morning, after a breakfast of French toast and fresh fruit delivered to their cabin, they ventured a walk through the woods surrounding the cabins, following a marked trail that meandered downhill, across a creek twice, and then circled back uphill toward the trail's starting point.

Robert realized the previous evening that his new wife had never succumbed to temptations of the flesh and had given herself wholly to him and no one prior. He pondered as they walked whether or not his failure to mention his past indiscretions constituted a sin of omission. His teen years had been filled with activities that went against the teachings of both his church and his parents, and the sealed court records allowed Robert and his best friend Kenny Gilbert to legally deny they were ever involved in the juvenile justice system. He had forsaken his violent past when he entered seminary, and his reward had been his own church, a beautiful bride, and a bright future serving the needs of his parishioners.

His reverie was interrupted by a large dog of indeterminate breed that charged barking and snarling through the woods from a neighboring property.

Frightened, Heather clung to Robert's arm.

Without thinking, he turned and pointed at the dog.

"Go home!" he commanded, in a voice best suited to casting out the Devil.

The dog stopped less than ten feet from them. Robert shook off Heather and strode purposefully toward the animal, still shouting. "Be gone!"

The dog turned and ran away through the woods.

When Robert returned to Heather's side, his new wife wrapped her arms around him and held him tight. Then she stretched up on her tiptoes, kissed him, and whispered, "My protector."

* * * *

The honeymoon was brief, and they returned home Monday morning. The wedding gifts were in the parsonage awaiting their return, and that afternoon they sat in the living room and opened them. Heather made careful notes about which gift came from which parishioner so that she could write personalized thank you notes to each of them. Having registered at a local department store, they found themselves with eight complete place settings of their chosen china, eight complete sets of flatware, numerous kitchen gadgets, and a variety of things they neither needed nor desired.

When they began opening the cards, making notes about the tens and twenties that fell out, Heather suddenly stopped and looked up at her husband.

"Bobby," she said, an expression of surprise mixed with concern on her face. She fanned out ten crisp one-hundred-dollar bills. "There's a thousand dollars in this one."

"Who's it from?"

"The card isn't signed," she said. "Who would have that kind of money?"

"In our congregation?" he asked. "No one I can think of."

"This is enough to repair my car," Heather said. She had drained her savings account to purchase her wedding dress, and student loan payments had prevented Robert from even opening a savings account.

They set the money and the card aside, intending to learn the identity of their anonymous benefactor so they could express proper thanks. They never did, though, and two weeks later Heather retrieved her car from the repair shop and drove it to the post office to mail thank you cards for all but one of their wedding gifts.

* * * *

Robert was in the church office one Wednesday, several weeks after his wedding, and he was drafting that Sunday's sermon when his private line rang. The church's telephone system was so old it didn't have Caller ID, and though the church secretary was supposed to screen incoming calls, too many people knew his private telephone number because the pastor's number had not changed since the system was installed. Each time Robert answered his private line he had an equal chance of finding himself speaking to a parishioner or a telephone solicitor. So, he took a deep breath and picked up the phone. "Pastor Bob."

A vaguely familiar voice said, "You're going to see an increase in tithing this Sunday."

"Thank you," Robert said, still unsure to whom he was speaking.

"Be mindful how you spend the money."

"Excuse me?"

But the caller said nothing more, and not until after the conversation ended did Robert realize where he previously heard the caller's voice. After all, he'd only heard it once before as a whisper in his ear.

Union Revival Baptist Church did not pass collection plates during Sunday service, instead relying on parishioners to slip their tithes into a pair of collection boxes mounted to the wall in the vestibule. Just as the caller predicted, the offering boxes were almost a thousand dollars heavier than usual that Sunday, and Robert sat in his office pondering what that might mean. Tithing was up again the following Sunday, and again the Sunday after that.

The church trustees were surprised at the unexpected surge in tithing and began to discuss how they might best spend the windfall. Robert suggested they not make hasty decisions, but during the following weeks, as the surge in tithing continued, the leaking roof was repaired, the parking lot resurfaced, and the parsonage's aging refrigerator replaced, much to Heather's delight. After taking care of the church's few needs, the trustees increased the congregation's donations to the interfaith food bank aiding the poor and homeless.

* * * *

Union Revival Baptist Church owned an entire city block. The church building occupied one end and the two-story parsonage, built of the same stone as the church, occupied the other. From his office window, Robert could see the parsonage, and he often found himself staring at it. What had once been a cold and lonely place foisted off on him by trustees unable to provide a housing allowance had been turned into a warm and welcoming home. After the previous pastor was killed in a hit-and-run accident, the parsonage had become his residence, replacing the one-bedroom garage apartment provided as part of his compensation package. Pastor John had done nothing to make the place welcoming during his decades-long tenure, and neither had Robert upon taking residence. Heather had overseen the transformation.

That's why Robert enjoyed walking home for lunch each day, even on days when heavy rain might have given him pause if he still lived alone. The walk to the parsonage cleared his mind of church business, and Heather often had lunch prepared, even if only a peanut butter and jelly sandwich accompanied by a cold glass of milk. They sat at the kitchen table sharing idle conversation, the subject matter less important than the company.

When Robert stepped through the door mid-day one Thursday, already salivating for the leftover meatloaf and mashed potatoes his wife promised him that morning, he was not prepared to find the curtains closed and the parsonage dark as the Middle Ages.

"Heather?" he called. "I'm home."

His wife rushed from the kitchen and into his arms.

Surprised, he asked, "What's wrong?"

"There's been a car parked across the street all morning."

Robert stepped to the living room window and looked out. "I don't see one now."

"The car drove away just before you came home," she said. "I saw it yesterday morning, too, but I didn't think anything about it until I saw it again today. I think someone is watching the house."

"But why?"

She had no idea.

"Why didn't you call me?"

"I was afraid I was imagining things," she said, "and I—I didn't want to bother you."

Robert kissed his wife's forehead. "You're never a bother."

He held her for a bit longer, waiting until he was certain she had calmed down, and then he asked, "How's that meatloaf?"

* * * *

That afternoon and all day Friday, Robert repeatedly checked the streets surrounding church property and not once did he see any unexpected vehicles parked near the parsonage. He was not nearly as attentive that weekend. Saturday he was busy with church business, and Sunday he led both the morning and the evening services, for they had yet to find an assistant pastor to fill the position he vacated upon his promotion. Robert had not minded the workload when he was single, for idle minds and idle hands were the Devil's playthings, but as a married man he had many more responsibilities. Those included attending to his spouse's physical and emotional needs.

At lunch Monday, after walking the long way around the block to get home, Robert asked Heather about the mysterious vehicle she had seen the previous week.

"I haven't seen it," she said. "I must have been mistaken."

But he knew she wasn't when he took a phone call in his office that afternoon. Though he had not heard it often, Robert recognized the voice in his ear.

"You've been pastor for almost a year and a half now, haven't you?"

Robert admitted that he had.

"You ever wonder how you got the job?"

He thought about the years spent in college and seminary, the grueling interviews he'd been put through when seeking his first position, and all the hard work he'd done as Union Revival Baptist Church's assistant pastor in the belief that God helps those who help themselves. When the church's beloved pastor was killed in a hit-and-run accident following a visit to one of the homebound parishioners, Robert had been fully prepared to ascend to the vacant position. The trustees and the congregation had agreed. Before he could form a response, though, he learned the answer.

"Pastor John had the courage of his convictions," said the voice. "He wouldn't work with us and we needed someone who would."

"You've been watching my wife."

"She's such a beautiful woman," said the voice. "It would be a shame if anything happened to her."

"You think you can use her to—"

"I know we can, pastor," said the voice. "Heather went shopping this afternoon. Perhaps you should check on her."

Before Robert could reply, the line went dead.

He immediately dialed his wife's cellphone number. He let it ring until Heather's voice mail answered. Then he hung up and tried again with the same result.

The moment he depressed the switchhook, his phone rang. He answered, his voice more irritated than welcoming. "Pastor Bob!"

"Is this Robert Connelly?"

"Who is this?" Robert demanded as he rose from his chair and stared out the window toward the parsonage.

The caller identified himself as a police detective and then said, "Your wife's been involved in an incident."

"An incident?" Robert demanded. "What does that mean?"

"You'd best come to the hospital."

Robert vacated his office without closing the open files on his computer, didn't bother turning out the lights or locking his office door, and was halfway down the front steps before calling over his shoulder to the church secretary who was trying to catch up to him. "Heather's been in an accident."

Only she hadn't.

The black eye, the bloody lip, and the bruises on her arm were the result of a mugging in the parking lot of a big box store where she had gone to purchase laundry detergent and frozen pizza.

By the time Robert found his wife in the emergency room, Heather had already described her assailants to the detectives, and had promised to visit the police station the next day to sign a statement and leaf through a selection of mug shots.

"He took my purse," Heather explained to her husband. "That wasn't enough for him, though. He had to do this, too." The mugger had temporarily stolen her beauty with several well-placed punches that were not life threatening.

Once they were in Robert's car, she had more to say. "He knew who I was. I told the police I didn't know who he was. I didn't. I don't. But he sure knew who I was, and he said he was sending you a message. What kind of message was he sending you, Bobby?"

"I don't know," he said, shading the truth just a little, uncertain if he was protecting his wife or protecting himself as they completed the trip home in silence.

Robert parked behind the parsonage and followed Heather through the back door into the kitchen.

She screamed.

He pushed past her, ready to do battle with whatever had frightened Heather, but saw only her purse in the middle of the kitchen table.

He turned to her. "I thought you said—"

"I did." She collapsed into his arms. "Why is it here? How did they get in?"

"Your keys were in your purse," he said, a simple explanation for the question easiest to answer.

When Heather calmed down, she upended her purse on the table and examined everything—her keys, her cellphone, her wallet, breath mints, pocket Bible, and an assortment of the detritus that accumulates in a purse not emptied regularly.

"Is anything missing?"

Heather shook her head. "Nothing. Nothing at all."

Then she insisted they change the locks, even though the keys to the parsonage were still on her key ring with all her other keys.

"They could have made duplicates."

Robert called a locksmith, a parishioner who promised to do the job that afternoon without charge once he learned why Robert desired the change.

* * * *

Heather was the center of attention at Wednesday evening's church service. She'd done her best to mask her bruises, blackened eye, and split lip, but the locksmith told his wife, she told everyone in the Women's Auxiliary, and from there the entire congregation heard about the mugging. Neither Robert nor his wife mentioned that the muggers had returned Heather's purse, letting everyone believe the reason for changing the locks was fear of some future home invasion.

Robert's sermon that evening was a variation on Matthew 5:39, where believers are admonished to turn the other cheek, even though the anger he felt inside demanded the exchange of an eye for an eye as advocated in Exodus 21:23-25.

He still felt that anger when the anonymous caller phoned the next day. Robert demanded, "What do you want?"

"Your cooperation," said the voice. "You know we can get to your wife anytime we want."

Robert repeated his question, "So, what do you want?"

"We're going to give a lot of money to your church, pastor. We just want to ensure that it gets spent wisely."

"The money comes in dirty and goes out clean?"

"Nothing's cleaner than God's hands."

"What does the church get out of it?"

"The church keeps ten percent," said the voice, "and we don't touch your wife."

Robert said nothing.

"We can push as much as a million dollars a year through Union Revival," said the voice. "Imagine the good you could do with an extra hundred grand each year."

"You know I can't do this alone." He started to explain that every check issued by the church for more than one thousand dollars required two signatures, Robert's and—

"Have a private conversation with your treasurer," the voice said before Robert could finish. "We know where his daughter attends college, and he knows that we know."

"Harvey wouldn't—"

"Who contracted with the roofer and the asphalt company?"

Harvey Johnson had made the recommendations to the board. "And the refrigerator?"

"We didn't make a cent on your refrigerator." The man on the other side of the conversation laughed. "We don't run an appliance store."

* * * *

Retired for almost ten years, Harvey Johnson had served as Union Revival Baptist Church's treasurer for almost thirty, and Robert cornered him after the monthly trustee meeting that evening.

"Why didn't you warn me at the wedding reception?"

"About what?"

"The man I asked you about, the one who spoke to me just before you did."

"I didn't see him," the treasurer insisted.

"He threatened my wife," Robert said. "He may have threatened your daughter."

"Alison's all I have." The church treasurer's only child had been born late in his life to a wife ten years his junior. Cancer had claimed Harvey's wife before his daughter ever entered kindergarten, and he had raised Alison on his own.

"Has he harmed her?"

Harvey didn't answer Robert's question directly. Instead, he asked one of his own. "Is that what happened to your wife?"

Robert nodded.

"I've never seen the man who threatened my daughter," Harvey explained. "He first approached me at Alison's high school graduation. He said I had a beautiful daughter and that it would be a shame if anything happened to her. By the time I turned to see who had spoken, he had disappeared into the crowd."

High school graduation ceremonies had been held two weeks before the pastor's wedding. "One other unusual thing happened that day," Harvey continued. "We held a little reception afterward, with family and friends. My daughter received several nice graduation gifts, including an unsigned card containing ten one-hundred-dollar bills. We never knew who to thank for the money, but we used it as a down payment on a used car for Alison."

Harvey hesitated so Robert prompted him to continue.

"Nothing happened all summer, so I forgot about everything. Then, just after the school year began, I received a call from campus police. My daughter had been mugged, her purse stolen. She wasn't hurt—not like your wife—just a few scrapes from being knocked down."

Harvey looked around to ensure they were still alone. Then he lowered his voice and leaned forward, as if sharing a secret with Robert. "Alison called later that night to say that when she returned to her dorm room, her purse was on her desk, as if she had left it there, even though she knew she hadn't. Then she told me one thing she hadn't told the campus police. She said her mugger told her he was sending a message to me."

"That he can get to your daughter anytime, anyplace."

Harvey nodded. "I've done what he wanted ever since."

"The roofer and the asphalt company?"

"He told me who to hire for those jobs. They weren't the lowest bidders by any stretch of the imagination."

"Have you talked to the police about any of this?"

"No. Have you?"

The two men stared at one another for a moment. Then Robert told Harvey's hands and said, "Let us pray for God's guidance."

* * * *

"The man who had you mugged wants to launder money through the church," Robert explained. He was sitting with his wife at the kitchen table in the parsonage, and he had to explain what it meant to launder money. "He threatened to hurt you if I didn't do what he said."

"He already hurt me, Bobby." Heather pushed her chair back and stood. "I thought you were my protector."

Robert reached for his wife's hand, but she turned away and left him sitting alone as she climbed the back stairs. He leaned back to stare Heavenward, but he did not pray. Instead, he followed the sound of his wife's footsteps until he heard the creak of their bed as she settled into it.

Then he took his cellphone from his pocket and dialed a number he memorized years earlier and had hoped to never dial.

* * * *

Thanks to its location near the heart of the city, its attention-getting imposing stone architecture, and its historical significance as the first church built in the valley, the Union Revival Baptist Church drew several visitors each Sunday. Some became members, some became regular attendees but never formally joined the church, and some were just passing through on their spiritual path. Regardless, all were welcome.

From the pulpit that Sunday, Robert barely recognized Kenny Gilbert when he slipped in at the last moment and, surprisingly, found an open seat in the back pew. Robert kept one eye on Kenny during the service and Kenny kept both eyes on everyone else. When they'd been released from juvenile detention, their lives diverged. With a fear of God not nearly as overpowering as a fear of his father, Robert straightened up, graduated high school a year late, and squeaked into college, where he majored in history and minored in English before attending seminary. Kenny traveled a different path into adulthood, one that found him solving physically the problems Robert attempted to solve spiritually.

Until Thursday evening, they had spoken only once since the day they walked out of juvie together. When Robert graduated from seminary, Kenny called to offer his congratulations and his personal cellphone number, a number Robert had memorized but hesitated to dial until he believed he had no other choice.

Though he barely listened to himself, Robert's message, inspired by Romans 12:19 and contradicting what was in his heart, was particularly inspiring that morning, and three people answered the call, publicly expressing their desire to devote their lives to God by joining him before the congregation. After speaking quietly to each of them, Robert introduced them to the congregation and then handed them off to a trio of deacons who silently joined them at the front. He closed the service with a prayer and then joined his wife in the vestibule.

Though Heather had been sleeping with her back to Robert since Thursday night, none but the most astute among the congregation could have ever suspected a rift between the pastor and his wife. In public they were still the bubbly, doe-eyed newlyweds, and they stood beside one another greeting parishioners as they exited the church.

Kenny held back, not approaching the pastor until most everyone else filed out. The two men shook hands, Robert introduced his childhood friend to his new wife without telling her the nature of their relationship, and then let Heather know they would have company at Sunday dinner.

"Pleased to make your acquaintance Mr. Gilbert," Heather said. "I trust you like pork chops and mashed potatoes."

"Ma'am," Kenny said. "I've not eaten a home-cooked meal in a great many years."

Before she could ask why, Robert directed his guest away from his wife, and the two men made their way to Robert's office. With the door closed, he repeated everything he'd told Kenny on the phone a few days earlier.

"It has to be an inside job," Robert explained. "Someone's using the offering envelopes to slip the money into the offering boxes. Each Sunday since the first call we've found ten crisp one-hundred-dollar bills folded neatly inside one of the envelopes."

A rap on the door interrupted their conversation, and then the church treasurer stepped into the office. He saw the pastor's guest and apologized. "But you wanted to know as soon as I collected the money from the offering boxes. There were two envelopes today."

"Thanks, Harvey."

After the treasurer backed out and closed the door, Robert said. "He's escalating."

"You said he could push a million dollars a year through the church," Kenny said. "Who has that kind of juice?"

"No one I know."

The two men talked a while longer, and then they walked to the parsonage, where Heather had set the dining room table with their wedding china.

After she carried the food to the table and the three of them settled into their seats, Robert said grace.

They ate in silence until Heather asked, "How do you know my husband?"

Kenny glanced at Robert before answering. "We grew up together."

"Really?" Heather asked, surprised. "He's told me so little about his childhood."

"There isn't much to tell," Kenny said. "We spent a lot of time indoors."

Imagining only one possible reason why her husband might have spent his teen years indoors, Heather looked at Robert and said, "You played a lot of video games?"

They had, in fact spent hours doing nothing but playing video games, and a great deal more time reflecting on the capriciousness of justice that led to their incarceration in a juvenile detention center for violent offenders but had not protected Kenny's little sister from the molester they crippled. When they were released, they chose different paths to combat evil.

"We did."

Robert interrupted before his wife could further question Kenny. "He's going to be staying with us for a while."

"Here?"

"No," Robert said, "in the garage apartment."

Then he asked his wife about the previous afternoon's Women's Auxiliary meeting, and soon she was telling the two men about the group's plans to expand membership. "We need to recruit more young women, and to do that we need an active social media presence."

Robert agreed, their conversation continued, and Heather never returned to questions about Robert's past or his relationship with Kenny.

When they finished the meal, Kenny thanked Heather and told her how much he enjoyed her cooking. "Robert's a lucky man."

As Heather cleared away the dishes, Robert gave Kenny a key to the empty garage apartment intended for the church's assistant pastor, and he didn't see Kenny again until morning service the following Sunday when he sat in the last pew watching the worshippers. At the end of the service he slipped out to follow a non-descript man who had been attending services at Union Revival Baptist Church since well before Robert and Heather's wedding.

Later, the church treasurer told Robert that anonymous tithing was up to five thousand dollars that morning. "Five envelopes, a thousand dollars in each."

"Did anyone see who put them in the collection box?"

"Most of the parishioners use the offering envelopes, so it's impossible to tell one from another."

"But five envelopes at once?"

* * * *

Robert was home Tuesday evening when a police detective visited his wife and showed her a photograph. "Is this the man who attacked you?"

"Yes," she said. She had previously identified her assailant from police mug shots. "I think so. It all happened so fast, but—yes. Have you arrested him?"

The detective shook his head. "He's been killed."

Heather's eyes went wide, and she glanced at her husband.

"Do you know anything about it?"

Heather shook her head.

"What about you, pastor?"

"God works in mysterious ways, detective," Robert said.

Satisfied, the detective left the parsonage. As the unmarked police car drove away, Robert gathered his wife in his arms and held her. "He can't ever hurt you again."

That night Heather stopped sleeping with her back to her husband.

* * * *

There were other deaths in the city that week, including that of the non-descript man Kenny followed from church service Sunday morning, but Robert paid attention to the obituaries when he scanned the newspaper each morning only if he had reason to believe he might be called upon to prepare a eulogy.

He returned to his office Friday afternoon, after lunch with his wife in the parsonage, and he was feeling rather full after finishing off the leftover roast beef, mashed potatoes, and gravy. He was considering the impropriety of taking a brief nap at his desk when his phone rang.

"Pastor Bob."

"We appear to be at an impasse," said a voice that had become all too familiar since his wedding many months earlier.

"How's that?"

"A friend of yours has asked me to place this call. He's under the impression I had something to do with your wife's unfortunate—"

Robert heard the nearly inaudible pop of a silenced automatic, though he did not recognize it as such. Then he heard Kenny's voice.

"It's done."

The line went dead.

Robert did not see Kenny again, and when he visited the garage apartment, it had been wiped clean.

During the following weeks, church trustees were disappointed that tithing had dropped to its previous level.

Police investigating the murder of a man with alleged mob ties never connected the dead man to Harvey Johnson or Robert Connelly, acting on the assumption that it was a hit by a rival mobster. However, after reading news stories about the murder and subsequent stalled investigation, Robert's wife finally put it together.

"I don't know what you and Kenny did," Heather told Robert one night after they slipped into bed, "and I don't want to know."

He pulled his wife into his arms and held her tight as she whispered, "My protector."

Michael Bracken has written several books, including the private eye novel *All White Girls*, and more than 1,300 short stories, including crime fiction published in *Alfred Hitchcock's Mystery Magazine*, *Black Cat Mystery Magazine*, *Ellery Queen's Mystery Magazine*, and *The Best American Mystery Stories*. As mentioned in the editorial, he just assumed sole editorship of *Black Cat Mystery Magazine* (although this story was purchased before he did so).

THE MAGNIFICENT SCORE

JOHN HEGENBERGER

The doorbell rang.

Which is weird, because my tiny office at the back of the Brown Derby restaurant has no doorbell. Neither does my forty-eight-foot boat moored at its slip in Santa Monica, for that matter.

"Ding. Dong. It's not Avon."

No, it was Norman Weirick fooling around again. I should have known. He'd been acting funny throughout all of 1959, since I'd taken him on as an "assistant" private investigator, and now in the early days of 1960, it looked like I was in for another year of his clever yet unpredictable shenanigans.

I shuffled a few papers around on my battered desk in order to appear busy. "Hey, buddy. What's doing?"

Norm dropped into the creaking client chair and adjusted the Coke-bottle lenses on the bridge of his nose. "MGM is trying to put United Artists out of business."

I couldn't help tightening my brow. It's something I often did when Norm obliquely started a conversation. Pretty soon after that, I usually got a headache. "The big studios are still reeling from the WGA strike. And they're always battling each other behind the scenes. So what's the big deal?"

He rolled the swivel chair forward two inches, right up to the front edge of my desk. "The big deal?" His voice was akin to that of a young screech owl. "The big deal is…."

The phone rang.

I raised a palm. "Hold that thought." Picking up the receiver, I gave out with my usual opening line. "Stan Wade, detective. How can I help?"

There was a muffled sound on the other end of the call. Then: "Uhm, is your refrigerator running?"

I hung up and looked eye-to-eye at Norm. "Go on."

Outside my office door, some poor soul dropped a tray of glassware. Slivers tinkled down the tile hallway, sliding out toward where the restaurant patrons ate lunch. *Just another typical day at the office.*

I returned my attention to Norman, who told me about director John

Sturges, whom I'd heard of due to the success of *The Old Man and the Sea.* He went on to reference film composer Miklos Rozsa, whom I'd *never* heard of, but should have due to the grandeur of his film score for *Ben-Hur*. I knew a lot about movies. Nonetheless, what I know about movie *music*, you can put in a piccolo.

My eyes were about to glaze, and then Norm mentioned that Steve Cromwell was leaning on Sturges. I'd had recent dealings with Cromwell while on a case up in Corriganville. Jack Warner's chief fixer had an underhanded technique of blackmailing the studio's actors to keep them under control. I'd tried to get evidence to disrupt this ploy, but he was mobbed up tight. I itched to go another round against him and this Sturges/Rozsa thing sounded like a perfect opportunity.

"So Sturges is making *The Magnificent Seven* at United Artists." Norm laced his fingers together on top of his burr haircut. "And he wants Rozsa to do the score." His elbows extended out to each side like a human TV antenna. "But Rozsa's under contract with MGM for the remake of *King of Kings*. He's stalled out inspirationwise and wants to moonlight with Sturges."

"Okay. I follow so far. What's this have to do with Cromwell?"

"MGM, by the way, would love to see UA fail, so they can buy them out."

"I'm not interested in corporate takeovers." I leaned back, accidently banging the top of my chair against the wall. My face must have given away my impatience. I hoped so.

"But imagine…." Norm lowered his arms and spread his hands wide over my desk, almost knocking over a stack of unpaid bills. "If one studio acquired or crippled all the others, they'd hold a monopoly over the industry. It'd be a nightmare."

"Where does Cromwell come into it?"

He swallowed, composing his thoughts for my benefit. "MGM doesn't want to spook Rozsa, so they've hired Cromwell to strongly convince Sturges to get someone else to write the film score. You follow?"

I straightened the pile of past due notices. "Force him how?"

"Ah, now here's the interesting part. Remember that red-headed lady found strangled and dumped in the bushes near the Arroyo High School a couple of years back?"

"No. And how do you know about all this?"

"Research. For my new novel. It's gonna be a western with werewolves."

I almost put a hand to my face. "What's your point, Norm?"

"My point is: Cromwell is threatening to tell the cops that he has evidence that Sturges was the killer."

"Does he?"

"I don't know." He slumped a fraction of an inch. "Sturges just wants Cromwell off his back so he can concentrate on his new movie. When I heard about it all, I immediately thought that you might…want to…look into it?"

"Indeed." It sounded like Steve Cromwell was up to his usual dirty tricks and that made me smile. "Yeah, I think I might." *But first I need a little research of my own.*

* * * *

I began by asking Suzi to look into Norm's story. I wanted to know more about Rozsa and Sturges. And what really interested me was the murder of the red-headed woman.

Suzi, my fiancée, ran her own investigations agency. We were partners in most senses of the word and planned to officially tie the knot in a few months. She had a couple of cracker-jack operatives who could track down info on Rozsa and Sturges, and I knew she would take a personal interest because of the murdered woman.

Usually all this would cost me an expensive dinner and floorshow, maybe at Earl Carroll's club, if it was still open. Under those conditions, Suzi would get me the facts, ma'am, *pro bono* on this case, or *moi bono*, if I knew Suzi. And I did.

Norman arranged a three o'clock meeting for me with John Sturges at the UA lot. As the director of *Last Train from Gun Hill* took my hand in greeting, I gave him my card and noticed that he never stopped moving. Tapping a pencil on the desktop. Shuffling through papers and glossy photos. An all-action sort of guy.

I took a seat on a couch half-covered with scripts and storyboard drawings, hoping it would settle him down. "I hear Cromwell is pressuring you to get a new composer."

He paced four steps back and forth in front of a shaded window that faced a duck pond. "Can you get him off my back?"

"I can try. If we work together on it."

His dark eyes darted to the window, as if searching for an image that might be used in a photo shoot. There was a muscular sense to his face that made him seem constantly serious.

"I'll take any help I can get against the leech. What'll it cost me?"

I smiled. *This is your lucky day.* "No charge. It's personal."

That stopped him in his tracks, running his fingers over the top of his head, as if to slick back the hair that wasn't there. "I don't want any trouble. I just want to make movies unencumbered, understand?"

I nodded agreement.

His voice was raspy, perhaps from barking too may orders on the film set. "MGM's *Ben-Hur* sucked all the ticket sales and profit out of the Christmas trade and left my *Never So Few* playing to empty houses." He started bouncing a baseball off the office wall. A real bundle of nerves.

"Yeah, I get it. From what I've heard, MGM wants to put UA out of business. So, why don't you relax and tell me the details about Cromwell?"

We talked for another ten minutes, and I honestly didn't learn anything that Norm and Suzi hadn't already told me. At least, with this preliminary visit, I'd made a positive impression on Sturges. It was time to move on to the main attraction, a face-to-face interview with Cromwell.

* * * *

Late that afternoon, during the drive over to MGM on Washington Boulevard, I listened to the news on the car radio. On this cold, clear Groundhog's Day of 1960, Senator Hubert Humphrey came out of his hole to say that the young, Catholic candidate for President, Jack Kennedy, was too young and too Catholic. I recalled that Suzi currently had an open case working for Kennedy's campaign. She'd told me last week while we were playing tennis that she'd uncovered some mighty interesting dope on Richard Nixon. However, that was her investigation; mine was here at MGM.

I met Norman at the august, ancient studio still in operation, despite the unions and independent film makers. The backlot had seen better times in earlier years while filming classics like *Gone With The Wind*, *Gaslight*, and *Singin' in the Rain*. Recently, it had appeared in a couple of TV episodes of *The Untouchables*, clearly on its way downhill.

A surprisingly strong wind blew the heat around us. I remembered taking a tour here once as a ten-year-old. My fifth-grade class had walked among this mysterious, colorful blend of exotic locations, surrounded by costumed performers and massive camera equipment. At the time, I'd wanted to run away and hide, so I could live here forever. Now, the building façades crowded in on each other, drab, plain, and dull.

I said something about it to Norm. He shuffled along behind me, hands in his pants pockets. "Location shooting is the new rage in Hollywood. Camera equipment these days is a lot more portable and easy to handle."

Something not so easy to handle was our meeting with Steve Cromwell. I was familiar with his kind of corporate underhandedness. He specialized in intimidation and extortion. For years, the Mob had wanted to get into the movie industry and currently the Fixer was as far as their influence extended…or so I believed.

I glanced at my watch. Quarter to four. *How had it gotten to be so late?*

A woman with cat-eye glasses ushered Norm and me into Cromwell's office. The room was cast in antique Spanish with nail-studded chairs, leather cushions and a gray-green olivewood desk.

The Fixer dressed like a corporate executive; what is commonly called an "Organization Man." Here in sunny Hollywood, he'd be much too warm in a gray flannel suit, so he wore a shiny blue three-piece of what's known as sharkskin.

Cromwell's teeth gleamed whiter than normal, as if they'd been retouched by the makeup department. His black hair sat plastered close to his head without any parting. His eyes were as cold as two dimes frozen in ice. In fact, they reminded me of those plastic novelty ice cubes with dead flies in the center.

We didn't shake hands.

I told him why we were here and what we knew. He didn't care. He set fire to a cigarette with a Zippo from his vest pocket and puffed smoke in my general direction, squinting. I knew he commonly twisted the truth and bullied people without remorse. He was a Mob bureaucrat who could extinguish my little private eye agency with a couple of phone calls…yet I didn't care.

Norm tried to act tough. "I've heard you're threatening John Sturges."

Cromwell blinked at him and flicked an ash. "Don't you have to be at work somewhere?"

My pal seemed stuck for a comeback, so I leaned forward. "Disney gave him the day off."

Somehow that gave Norm a shot of babbling courage. "Yeah, and you accused the director of murdering some…some red-headed hooker last seen alive after midnight back in June of '58."

The Org Man looked at me and took a deep drag. "No idea what you two are talking about, Wade." He exhaled. "But you better knock it off."

It was a flimsy, magnificent challenge on Norm's part. Bluff the bluffer. Unfortunately, we all knew that the L.A. County Sheriff's department had no active suspect, so if Cromwell fingered Sturges, the cops would quickly land on the director.

Norman went on now to pretend that Sturges had been with him the night of the murder, working on a new piece of camera equipment. "It'll pan automatically during a wide shot from a moving vehicle."

I could see that Cromwell still wasn't buying it. He stared at us rigidly. *What does he know that we don't?*

His face became darker. He was about to speak, when, without knocking, the middle-aged woman with cat-eye glasses came into the office. "JR wants you." She acted as if Norm and I weren't there.

Cromwell got up and straightened his vest, keeping his eyes on us. "You should be leaving, fellas." He moved around the side of the desk, heading for the door and leaving his cigarette burning in an ashtray.

I got up, too. "Yeah." I reached over and crushed out his butt. *Tough guy to tough guy.* "We've got a crime scene to visit."

* * * *

From reports in the newspapers from June 23, 1958, we could see photos of the woman's son, Jimmy, and the location where the body had been found by a guy walking his dog late at night. Jimmy looked disconnected from events, too young to fully comprehend what had happened to his mother. According to the newspapers, she'd last been seen alive at the Desert Inn in El Monte.

There was no sign of her here now, a year and a half later. A clump of bushes had grown into the thicket where her body had lain. The gravel path next to the fence containing the athletic field still seemed to carry the trampled imprints from a troop of flat feet. Searching the area where the dead woman had been discovered only gave Norm and me a wrapper from a 5th Avenue candy bar and an empty RC Cola bottle.

My friend hung onto the bottle. "Two cents deposit."

I scanned the empty baseball field, watching a breeze push a stand of short pine trees back and forth. I was tempted to wave back. The twilight clouds raced along a darkening horizon. "Looks like it's fixin' to rain." Within the shadows below the trees, I thought for a moment I saw a deer with frightened eyes, but it bounded away. *Probably just a dog.*

Off in the distant row of cheap houses that backed up to the school lot, someone hammered. It was a little late in the day for putting up aluminum siding, but I could see two men in overalls climbing down a scaffolding to pack up their tools.

A piece of grit blew into my left eye. I rubbed it and let it water, enduring blurred vision for a couple of seconds. Thinking of the woman who'd been dumped at this innocent site, I wondered if all of reality was simply a blurred vision, like a ghostly half-moon drifting among clouds, a big nowhere.

Norm nudged me awake. "You wanna getoddahere?"

I took a breath and let it escape. "Yep."

* * * *

In my line of work, sometimes you have to just push stuff together or noodle around, before something important happens. Thus, late next morning, Norman and I drove across town to El Monte. Bobby Darin sang "Mack the Knife" on the car radio to which Norm snapped his fingers. I'd grown sick of hearing the song weeks ago, so I switched stations to catch the news. Some Negro students were staging a sit-in at a Woolworth's drug store in North Carolina. Hoagy Carmichael was scheduled to appear on tonight's episode of *Laramie* and Andy Griffith would be a guest on *The Garry Moore Show*. The USA had sent up a weather satellite that Norm swore was actually designed to spy on the Russians.

I found the Desert Inn on the south side of the street and parked my Thunderbird in the lot next to the entrance. Norm and I stepped inside to find the place almost empty. Beyond the restaurant's wide windows, the traffic on East Valley Boulevard hummed both ways. *Clearly a breakfast spot in the mornings and a watering hole at night.*

The long bar in the back of the low-roofed building gleamed from polished brass and backlit bottles. Leather chaps were nailed to the wall over the fireplace housing fake white birch gas-fired logs. Twin chandeliers fashioned from old wagon wheels hung horizontally over the plush booths. Little cowboy hats and boots decorated the napkins.

"I'll be darned. I think I just remembered this joint." Norm slid into the end booth and held up his hands as if he were taking pictures with an invisible camera. "This is where I snapped shots of Brando meeting a guy to pay off the Santa Anita bet."

A middle-aged, middle-weight cowgirl wearing a cap gun in a plastic holster ambled over to take our order. Her Desert Inn name tag said, "Large Marg." The laminated menu didn't offer much more than steak and eggs, Texas style, whatever that was.

Norm rubbed his palms together in anticipation. "I'm thirsty. Bourbon and branch water."

She popped her gum. "Oh, getting in the mood of things, huh?"

My friend grinned and pushed his glasses up his nose. "I'll take that as a compliment."

I wasn't sure where their conversation was going and didn't try to sort it out. Norm is often weird, like I said, and causes me to get a headache. "Coffee and OJ. No, make that a club soda and lime, please."

She scribbled on her order pad. "You a friend of Bill W?"

"No. Just him." I jerked a thumb at Norm. "And like him, I'm thirsty."

She scowled and popped gum again. "Coming right up."

I caught a strong whiff of Tabasco sauce blended with cigar smoke from two booths over, where a couple of beefy geezers scarfed down ham and eggs. No one was at the bar, this time of day.

"Right there." Norm gestured over by the phone booth. "Brando was standing right there and he had no idea I was taking pictures with my Minox spy camera. I got lots of shots of him paying off the...." His voice drifted away.

I looked up at him and saw that his mind was a million miles away.

He screwed up one side of his face in an evil grin. "I think I just solved the case."

* * * *

"You kept the negatives?"

We stood in the semi-dark of Norm's cluttered rental home near the new Dodger Stadium.

"Look around. I keep everything." Norm sloshed the fluids in a metal pan under the red light that hung above the sink. "Some of my old comic books will be worth a fortune before you know it."

I leaned over his shoulder to study the image developing on the 8 x 10 and caught a lung full of rank chemical fumes. "How'd you get these photos without anyone noticing?" I stifled a cough.

"The mini-camera was inserted in the spine of my hardback edition of *Tarzan and the Ant Men*."

Of course it was.

He held a dripping photo up with a pair of metal tongs. "Look. See that couple standing at the bar behind Brando? That guy next to the hot chick is Cromwell, right?"

A smudged and blurred man had an arm around the same woman I'd seen in the newspaper photos. She'd been seen with a man at the Desert Inn hours before her body was found in the field beside the high school. The cops never knew what the guy looked like for sure. Squinting now at Norman's photo, neither did I. "This is a mess, Norm. We can't make positive ID of Cromwell based on this fuzzy image."

"No. But the wickedly cool thing is, he doesn't know that." He waggled his eyebrows like Groucho. "Lemme see what I can do to fix the photo, so you can bluff him. I saw them do that trick on *77 Sunset Strip* once, and the guy confessed all over himself."

Yep, Norm is a little weird at times, but he'd saved my life last year during a case involving Ian Fleming. And I desperately wanted to get the goods on Cromwell. So much so, that it almost made my mouth water, as much as my eyes were from the pan full of chemicals. So, yeah, maybe a bluff *was* worth a try. "Where's your phone?"

"Over there, next to the ham radio."

For a scientific guy, Norm surprised me by having an old candlestick telephone, made of brass with a dial on it. I hefted it the way Bogart would have and called Cromwell's number at MGM. When he came on the line, I again tried to convince him that Sturges had an iron-clad alibi. I couldn't understand why the Fixer was trying to incriminate the director, instead of the composer.

"Simple, Wade." The enforcer's voice came back. "The studio doesn't want to come down hard on the orchestra guy. They need him to cooperate and perform at his best, so they sent me to stop Sturges from using him after hours on the side. You understand."

I didn't like being lectured to. "I've got news for you, Cromwell. You were seen at the Desert Inn with the redhead. We happen to have photographic proof from that night. We can pin the murder on you, or you can back off Sturges. Your call."

I was attempting to blackmail a blackmailer. In a way, it made us somewhat alike. *Forget that!*

The line went quiet for a heartbeat. "I've got to be at the Hollywood Bowl in three hours, fella, to check out security in the area." He sounded bored, and yet I caught an edge in his voice. "Meet me there with your so-called evidence and we'll talk."

I hung the receiver back on the hook and looked at it as though the Fixer's voice lived inside it. Then, I got to work.

* * * *

Despite frequent indications to the contrary, I'm not stupid. And up to now, Norm probably could have handled the entire case all by himself, but the circumstances were turning dangerous, which meant it was time for me to take full control. I also took a couple of precautions before heading out for the Bowl.

Last October, I'd attended a Moonlight Jazz concert here at the amphitheater. Thelonious Monk and Sarah Vaughan had played long into the night under the stars, accompanied by Count Basie's orchestra. I wondered what Rozsa thought of hot jazz.

As I drove up Highland Avenue north of Hollywood Boulevard, I passed a backhoe digging a trench along the side of the road to help drain off water from the recently installed fountains in front of the concert shell.

Cromwell and I met in one of the picnic grounds beneath the low-hanging palm trees. The pale blue shell of the amphitheater looked like the entrance to a man-made cave set near the side of the Hollywood Hills.

I didn't plan on getting into a fight with him. I found Cromwell leaning elegantly against the side of his Caddy, putting the flame of his Zippo to another cigarette.

I gave him my story and a look at the photos that Norman had hastily re-touched. From the flash in his eyes, I knew I'd hit pay dirt. *So he was there. And he's buying it.* I showed him the negatives as proof of good faith.

He inhaled deeply, tossed away the cigarette and reached for the film.

The flames from his discarded fag crackled in the dry brush beside us. Cromwell didn't seem to care. It had been a hot spring and a hotter summer, scorching the foliage and baking the earth throughout the area around the Hollywood Bowl.

I backed up not having planned on a forest fire. If we didn't stop it quickly, the whole hillside soon would be burning. A stiff wind now could feed a wild fire, baking, burning, and destroying everything for acres in every direction.

When I looked back at Cromwell, he had a black gun on me. "Give."

The flames crawled across the trail behind him.

I stood there with my hands raised, just like in some cheap cowboy or gangster picture. A gangster picture where I'd be the victim. *Firestorm at the Hollywood Bowl.*

"You know…." I stretched my neck to keep an eye on the fire growing behind him. "We're both in big trouble here."

He ignored the sounds of the flames. It dawned on me that maybe he'd planned the fire all along. *It'll cover my burnt remains after he shoots me.*

I had to stall him off or distract him somehow. I tried another bluff. "Like you, I've been around the track a few times and have contacts in the cops and FBI. Each of them is holding a sealed envelope with copies of these photos, so you'd be wise to plan a long trip out of the country."

The .38 in his fist drifted slightly to the left as he sighed. "Bullshit."

A burning branch tumbled down a slope setting fire to a patch of brambles. A brown rabbit leapt and scampered away.

He came forward and felt in my coat pockets, under my arms. Circling around, he patted my hips and waistband.

The heat became intense. The flames licked along the edge of the path where we stood and rippled up a vine-wrapped tree trunk.

I scanned the area but saw no one coming or going. "So, I guess we should head out, eh?"

"Down on your knees."

I didn't move, knowing that if I did, I wouldn't ever be getting back up again.

He slammed the left side of my head with the flat of his automatic and I slumped.

He came closer. "I'm going to enjoy this."

Fire danced high behind him. Dark smoke rolled over my face. He reached out and caught me by the necktie. My right hand dangled loosely beside my left foot. The Ruger .22 came out of my trousers from my left ankle.

His eyes widened. *He's going to shoot.*

A huge plume of hissing gas blew up from a fallen log. The flare caught his attention enough that I swung my left fist up under his chin. He went down like a bag of beach sand. I grabbed for his gun. It went off next to my right cheek. Lancing pain pierced my ear. I couldn't hear a thing. I waved my pistol around wildly, unable to find him in the vortex of flame and swirling darkness. Burning leaves drifted down into my face and hair.

Suzi had been my backup, watching through binoculars from further up the hill. It never occurred to either of us that Cromwell would be stupid enough to start a fire. By the time she got to me, my ears were ringing and my face felt like a mask of peeled flesh.

In the glut of roiling soot and heat, we couldn't find Cromwell's Caddy, but I caught sight of a string of silent fire trucks rounding the curve in the parking lot. Suzi got me into the back seat of my T-bird and sped us down the hill through clouds of dense smoke.

* * * *

I learned a major lesson that day: never back a rat into a corner. You just might find that you're the one who is trapped.

When we got to Hollywood and Vine and rode the elevator up to Suzi's offices in the Taft Building, she washed the blood from my ear, kissed me firmly and forced me to go to a local clinic for vision and hearing tests. The doctor there patched the side of my head and wrote out the word "tinnitus" on a prescription pad. I told Suzi I felt fine and she punched me in the stomach, knocking my breath out.

Hours later, we learned that the fire had been quickly contained. Someone had used a nearby backhoe to re-direct the flow of the fountain water from in front of the stage to help extinguish the flames.

Suzi inspected my bandaged head and spoke directly into my face, slowly. "You could have died in all that chaos, Standy."

I struggled to read her lips. "I love it when you call me that pet name."

She smiled and sighed.

"Cromwell let me live. I'm sure that means he bought my story about copies of the photos being held by the FBI. I've got an edge on him now and I'm going to find the best way to put him out of business."

Suzi called Sturges to relay the news that the Fixer probably no longer posed a serious threat. Next, I wanted to let Rozsa know that he could go ahead with the score for *The Magnificent Seven* movie. She liked the idea of meeting the music man in person, so I got high-jacked to his suite at the Bel-Air. *What the hell. Why not?*

Rozsa had a beautiful set of rooms in the hotel up Stone Canyon Road. MGM always goes first class. The suite was decorated in garden colors, and sunlight streamed in through shear curtains. Through an open window came a cool breeze and the laughing sounds from a swimming pool two stories below.

When I entered, Rozsa was absorbed in playing something on the piano. His fingers scampered over the keys in a simple pattern that faintly soared. Despite the ringing in my ears, I recognized a sort of combination between the thumping theme from *The Killers* and the race music from *Ben-Hur*.

I let him go on for a bit, even though my head ached like hell. Suzi stood there smiling, taking in the rhapsody that hurt my ear. Finally, I reached out and interrupted, which was a bad thing, since it set him off wandering the room with his hands behind his back. His stare reminded me of Peter Lorre. His stature and size were similar to the actor's, but with a softness and sensitivity around the mouth that put me at ease.

I clasped him by the shoulders. "I want you to understand that Cromwell is completely blocked. Things are fine with Sturges now. He wants you back on the score for his western. And I'm pretty sure MGM won't have a problem with it anymore."

He dropped down onto a pastel green and yellow davenport and folded one hand over the other in his lap. "It is you who does not understand at all."

I looked at Suzi and then back at the composer, who had jumped back up. "The head of production and other top studio executives at MGM are threatening *me* now over my exclusive contract."

For a little guy, he could poke you in the chest with a stiff finger hard enough to make you sit down. "You may have fixed things up with Sturges's problems, but I have the problems now."

"I'm not sure I heard you correctly."

His mouth moved slowly. "Attorney problems."

So.

Even if I'd gotten Cromwell to end the trumped-up charge against Sturges, the studio was taking a new tactic of threatening Rozsa.

The composer reached out to touch my upper arm, as if to steady himself, or to lend me a bit of his inspiration. "Besides, I don't like the score for this magnificent seven, so much. You heard it when you came in just now. It's all so lumpy-jumpy horsey-back riding." A vein swelled in his neck. His hands went up. "I've lost my muse. He can have it." Rozsa poked at my chest again. "Give it to Benny Hermann or Raskin or someone. I don't want my name on it."

I didn't understand a lot of that until later, but I saw Suzi poke her own finger at the little man and form one word with her firm lips: "Jerk."

* * * *

Weeks later, for reasons I may or may not have been a part of, MGM backed off its direct attempt to put UA out of business. They also backed off pressuring Sturges, for reasons I was sure I'd been a part of. I figured Cromwell was on a short leash, probably hiding out somewhere, waiting for our next go around. *Bring it on, fella.*

After finishing location shooting in Mexico, Sturges and his whole crew were back in town and had set up filming interior scenes at the Goldwyn Studios on Santa Monica Boulevard.

Norm wanted to go to the West Hollywood location, so he could meet Yul Brynner. I couldn't have cared less. I was just happy to see Steve McQueen again, who introduced me to his friend and fellow actor, James Coburn. The five of us, without Yul, ate dinner across the street at the Formosa Café. Sinatra sat at a dark table near the back with a very cute brunette. He raised his chin in greeting when he saw me and mouthed the single, friendly word, "Pally." I wiggled two fingers and having waved, moved on.

Sturges briefly took me aside and tried to thank me for getting him out of the murder frame. He ended up by giving me his pass to the studio and indicating that I could use it anytime. I ended up giving it to Norm, who kissed it.

Several courses of Chinese cuisine and rounds of drinks later, the director led us back to the UA screening room where we watched rushes from earlier that week. The scenes on the screen were a jumble, apparently making profound sense to the rest of the crowd.

Charles Bronson caught up with the gang around midnight and brought along Elmer Bernstein. The musician played a tune on a battered piano old enough to have accompanied Chaplin and Fairbanks during the silent era. "That, gentlemen, is the main theme from the film," Bernstein informed us.

No one in the room had heard it before, except me. They all gave a rousing cheer to the galloping Copland swing of the piece and passed around a bottle of Four Roses. Sturges immediately claimed that the sweeping theme would surely win an Oscar.

Maybe because of my weakened auditory nerve, I had the eerie feeling that I'd heard the tune once before...when Rozsa had played it at the Bel-Air. I kept the original composer's confidence and said nothing to the gang that night. And damned if the score didn't win at the next Academy Award ceremony ten months later. Which is about how long it took me to stop that lonely, weedy crime scene at the high school from haunting my dreams.

Still, every so often, I get brief flashes in my mind of those grainy newspaper photos of Jean Ellory's cold body lying there in the brush and the expressionless look in the eyes of her son, Jimmy.

Award-winning author John Hegenberger has produced more than a dozen books since mid-2015, including several popular series: Stan Wade, LA PI in 1959, Eliot Cross, Columbus-based PI in 1988, and Tripleye, the first PI agency on Mars. His latest novel, *The Pandora Block*, is a high-tech, international thriller. Several of his short stories have appeared in *Black Cat Mystery Magazine*. His Stan Wade, LA PI novel, *Spyfall*, won a 2016 award at Killer Nashville.

WORSE THAN DEATH
ROBERT LOPRESTI

"They have my son."

Luis Suarez's eyes went wide. "Teo?"

"How many sons do you think I have, you idiot?" snapped Maximilian Hidalgo. "Of course Teo!"

Suarez swallowed. The president was furious, and he had just made himself a target. *Don't panic. He needs you.*

"How did you find out?"

"Not from my head of security! No. I had to depend on the kindness of the kidnappers for that." He paused. "How did they get my private phone number?"

The great man was not thinking clearly. That made him even more dangerous than usual.

Suarez had been getting ready for bed when he was ordered to the presidential palace. For years he had assumed his death would follow such a call.

But not as long as he was useful.

"They have Teo's phone," he explained.

"Oh. Of course." Hidalgo ran his hands through his thick, unruly hair. He was an impressive man, tall and broad-shouldered. He looked like a leader, which Suarez thought was half the battle. Suarez was short and dumpy and knew he looked like a corrupt small-town cop.

The president was in his dressing gown, fine silk, royal blue. He was pacing around his small library, where only a few trusted advisers ever set foot.

"What did the kidnappers say?"

"Only that they had my son and I should prepare to hear their demands."

"Did you speak to Teo?"

The president looked blank and then went pale. "Are you saying he might be dead?"

"I'm asking if you are sure he was kidnapped at all." Suarez ran through his mental diary. "He was supposed to be visiting his cousins in Coracal, wasn't he?"

"Yes. I called them. My sister said Teo left just after dinner with his bodyguards." Hidalgo's head, which had been slumping forward, jerked up. "And where are they, damn them? If my son is gone, where the hell are your bodyguards?"

Suarez was careful to stay neutral, not to get defensive. "Three possibilities. They might have been killed by the kidnappers. Or, perhaps they were the kidnappers."

"My God," moaned the president. "You hired them, Luis!"

He nodded. "I don't believe they betrayed you, sir. But we have to consider every possibility."

"Yes, yes. Go on."

"Third, they were overpowered and the boy was taken, so they ran away."

"Why would they do that?"

"Fear of punishment, sir."

"Oh. Of course. What are you doing?"

Suarez had his phone out. "I will get men looking for the guards. If they are alive and free, they probably went home for money and possessions before they fled."

"Don't tell anyone Teo is missing!"

"No, sir." Not that a secret like that would keep for long.

* * * *

By the time Suarez was off the phone, Hidalgo had opened his vault. Suarez had known that a section of bookcase swung away to reveal the door, but he had never seen it open. The fact that Hidalgo had done so in front of him was one more indication of his state of mind.

Suarez was careful to stand still, letting the door block his view of the vault's interior. Showing too much interest would be a mistake.

"What is the going fee?" asked Hidalgo absent-mindedly from inside the vault. He laughed ruefully. "I am afraid I do not keep track of such marketing trends."

Suarez thought of recent reports of kidnappings in this part of the world. He named a figure that was many times more than he would see in his lifetime. "But that was for a prime minister. Not a president's son."

"I could pay that much," said Hidalgo, mostly to himself. "I would need to access many bank accounts. Much above that I will have to tap my foreign funds. How much time will they give me?"

"Speed is to their advantage. Also to Teo's."

"Teo, my God. Teo." Hidalgo walked out of the vault, his eyes unfocussed.

Suarez knew he needed to keep Hidalgo from sinking into a pool of terror. "Where's your phone, sir?"

"My what?"

"The phone they called. We need to put a trace on it."

"Oh. Yes. Do it!"

A little spark of the real man there. But he was still not fit for public view, so Suarez asked him to go to the bedroom when the technician arrived to work on the phone. "It wouldn't do for the people to see you—so concerned, sir."

While the technician worked, Suarez summoned Borges, a tiny man with an oversized skull. His laptop had the most complete file of terrorists and rebels in the country.

"Set up over there," Suarez told him, pointing to the far corner of the library. "And get me a list of all threats against the president's son."

Borges's eyes went wide. He opened his mouth to speak, but apparently thought better of it. He nodded and set to work.

Paca, Suarez's assistant, called back. Two of the guards had been spotted by neighbors leaving their homes with bags or suitcases. They had been in a hurry.

If the guards had been conspirators, they would have made sure they didn't need to go home. Most likely they had been overpowered and fled. The other two guards had been smarter and fled empty-handed. Panicked and pauperized exile was better than anything the president would have in store for them.

"Watch the borders," he told Paca. "And the airports and harbors. They are all fleeing."

* * * *

By the time the kidnappers called again, things were ready. When the president picked up the phone, a recorder was going, a trace was being made, and Suarez was on a silent extension.

"Yes?"

"Hello, Colonel." The voice was crisp, educated. The tone, mocking. Hidalgo had not reached the rank of general before a coup thrust him into power. Some dissidents assumed that title rankled, so *colonel* was a deliberate insult. Suarez didn't believe the president gave a damn about such matters, but since any insult to him was a capital offense, it made little difference.

"What have you done with my boy?"

"Little Teo? He's right here. I believe he wants to speak with you."

There was a sound of struggle. "Papa! I want to go home!"

Hidalgo gripped his hair as if to tear it out by the roots. "Teo! Be strong, son! I will save you, I swear it."

The educated voice was back. "Stop posturing, Colonel. The boy is back in his home-away-from-home."

"You bastard! If you harm a hair on his head—"

"You'll kill me? And what will you do if I *don't*?"

Hidalgo was silent, except for his panting.

"You'll kill me anyway, won't you?" The voice laughed. "You see, Colonel, that's the problem with your system. When you burn down a village because someone wrote a slogan on a wall, people think that if they are going to die anyway, so it might as well be for something more important. You understand?"

Hidalgo said nothing.

"But I promise you, your son will not be killed. We are not murderers. You are. Say it."

"Say what?"

"Say that you are a murderer."

"I will not play your—"

"Very well. The next sound you hear will be your boy screaming. I hope you have a strong stomach—"

"All right!" Hidalgo's right hand squeezed the phone. His left was a fist, held in front of his heart, and trembling. "I am a murderer."

"There!" The kidnapper sniffed, and that seemed to Suarez it was a gesture he used to gather his dignity. "Not so hard, was it? This will be easier if you don't pretend you have choices."

Hidalgo's voice was cold. "What do I have to do?"

"Ah! The practical man at last. I won't keep you in suspense, Colonel. We don't want any money. Not a centavo. All we want is your confession."

Hidalgo had been staring at the far wall as he listened but now he turned, eyebrows raised. *What do you make of this?*

Suarez could only shrug and point at the phone. *Keep him talking.*

"My confession? What do you mean?"

"You're going to write down a list of all your crimes against our people. Then you're going to send it to us."

"I have committed no crimes—"

"If you say that again…." The voice cracked.

Dangerous, Suarez thought. Under that educated veneer was a brutal man hungering to hurt someone.

"If you say that again, Colonel, your son will pay for it. Do you understand?"

Hidalgo licked his lips. "Yes."

"Excellent. We have already made up a list of your crimes and it is very complete. Ha! As far as we know. So when you send us *your* list we will compare. If you have left something off, little Teo will suffer for it."

"You said you would not kill him."

"A child can live without a finger or a toe, Colonel. Or without many of them. But you know that, don't you? There are many crippled beggars in the streets who owe their occupations to your interrogation methods."

The president collapsed into a chair. "We— You and I may not agree on what is a crime."

Another laugh. "Too true, Colonel! I will make that easy on you. I am only interested in wrongful deaths. Not torture, not robbery, not false imprisonment. Or graft, of course! My God, if we tried to cover all your sins, poor Teo would die of old age, wouldn't he?"

Suarez watched Hidalgo swallow hard. "You can't expect me to know all the names of, of..."

"You never wanted to know them, did you? No. All you have to do is write that on such-and-such a day my government ordered the village of Santa So-and-so torched. We estimate this-many men, women and children died. Easy, no?"

Suarez whispered a query to the tech man who sat at a keyboard, frustration burning on his face.

"We're getting locations, chief," the man said, "but they change every minute or two. These people have sophisticated technology."

"So you can't tell anything about their site?"

"They are in the country."

"Three days from tonight, Colonel," said the kidnapper. "You email me the list by 9 p.m. on Sunday. If it is complete, the boy will be released unharmed. If not— Well. What happens to him depends on how many tries it takes you to correct it."

"You will die for this," said Hidalgo.

"Better than dying for nothing."

"I will prepare your damned document. What will happen to my son in the mean time?"

Another chuckle. "Are you familiar with the phrase 'a fate worse than death?'"

Hidalgo went so rigid Suarez thought he would drop the phone. "Yes."

"Well, think worse than that, Colonel. Much worse."

"If you harm one hair—"

But he was shouting into a dead phone.

* * * *

"Are you going to kill me?"

Teo blurted it out as soon as the man walked in. He was a short man, balding and pudgy, older than Teo's father.

"No. Didn't the ones who brought you here tell you that?"

"Yes, but they all wore masks so I couldn't iden— iden—" He couldn't remember the word. "So I couldn't say who they are. You're letting me see your face, so you must not think I will have a chance to— to—"

"Identify." The man sniffed, which made him look irritable. Then he smiled. "No one is going to kill you, Teo. I wear no mask because if we succeed no one will try to punish me. If we fail, your father will certainly find me whether you see my face or not."

"Succeed at what? Fail at what?"

The man sat down. There were two plain wooden chairs in the room along with a simple bed, a stinking toilet and a sink. There was also a table and, next to it, a small bookcase.

There were no windows and only one door.

"We are trying to accomplish two things, Teo. My name is Alberto, by the way. One of them is to persuade your father to do a certain thing."

"My father will never give in to terrorists!"

Alberto frowned. Then he gave a hoarse laugh. "I was going to say we are not terrorists, but I suppose we are, yes? We want to bring terror to your father's heart. But usually when people talk about terrorists, they mean people who attack civilians. Innocent bystanders."

"I am a civilian!"

"Not at all. You are a member of the ruling regime. One of its most important parts, actually."

Teo felt tears filling his eyes. "I want to go home!"

"You will, I assure you. No one here means you any harm."

"Then let me go!"

Alberto sighed. "You are not ready yet. First you must learn the truth about your father."

"What do you mean? I know all about him. He is a great man!"

"No." The voice was flat and cold. Alberto walked to the door and knocked. "We are ready, I think."

The man who came in was wearing a bandanna over his face, like a bandit in a movie, but other than that he was dressed like a thousand peasants Teo had seen outside the palace. His droopy hat and the bandanna covered everything but his eyes.

His head tilted slightly as if Teo were a strange phenomenon that needed careful consideration.

"What do you want?" the boy asked.

"My son was eleven," said the man. "Your age, but not nearly as big as you. I couldn't feed him very well."

"That's not my fault!"

"Of course not," said Alberto. "Tell him what happened to your boy."

"He went to town one market day. He wanted to buy a chicken of his own to raise. He had saved his money." Again, the tilted head. "Have you ever saved money for something?"

Teo didn't answer.

"Your father was coming through our village on the way to, I don't know, somewhere more important. One of his army trucks arrived first, clearing the way. My son didn't move fast enough, and they ran him down."

Teo squeezed his hands tight. "I'm very sorry. But what does that have to do with me?"

"The men stopped to help my boy. Your father's car came along, and he yelled at the men to get back in the truck. Said he was going to be late."

"I'm sorry," Teo said again. His voice quavered.

"My son died. They could have easily taken him to the hospital."

The boy said nothing.

When the man left Teo turned to Alberto. "That's just a story. It might not even be true. What do you expect me to say?"

"I expect you to listen." He knocked on the door, a sound that Teo would learn to dread.

An old woman came in. She was stooped and gray and had not bothered with a bandanna. She squinted at Teo with rheumy eyes. "Your father killed my husband."

"Have a seat, Señora," said Alberto. "You might as well, too, Teo. Many people wish to talk to you."

* * * *

At five in the morning, they found one of the bodyguards in the back of a smuggler's truck. Border guards brought him to the police headquarters next to the palace.

The prisoner was handcuffed and had bruises on his face and arms.

The guards assured Suarez that they hadn't done any intentional harm. "But he fought like the devil was waiting for him."

Suarez didn't blame the man.

"Get a doctor." He stepped into the cell, carrying a chair.

The guard was on the floor, half sprawled against a wall. His hands were cuffed behind his back and one ankle was chained to a bracket in the floor.

"Eduardo, my friend, what happened?"

"I have no friends." The voice was a croak. "Why should I talk to you? Dead men don't talk."

Suarez sat down.

"You aren't dead."

"Don't pretend I have a chance to live through this."

"You don't. But there are better and worse ways of dying." Suarez paused. Should he mention the man's wife? No, if he applied too much pressure, he wouldn't trust the answers he got.

"I always thought you were a man who respected his duty, Eduardo." Silence.

"Your duty is still to protect the boy. Nothing has changed."

The guard shuddered. "I failed."

"That is no excuse for failing again. Tell me what I need to know to save the boy. Which of your detail was the inside man? Was it you?"

"No! None of us!"

"There had to be one. How else could they have known where you would be?"

Silence.

"You took a different route every time you went to the cousins, yes? That is standard procedure." Their estate was well guarded, but the roads, of course, were not.

"We did. We did. But…"

Suarez felt his shoulders sag. *There it is.* All the training and security measures in the world, defeated by a single word. *But…*

"Where did you go?"

"We stopped every time at Estriba."

Suarez frowned. "That little village in the foothills? What's there for you? Women? Gambling?"

The guard had enough dignity left to scowl with his one open eye. "Never! Not when the boy was with us!"

"Then what?"

Silence.

"Damn it! Do I have to beat it out of you? Do your duty!"

"Pastry!" Eduardo was shaking with something. Anger. Embarrassment. "There is a stand there that sells *alfajores*. Teo liked them so much he begged us to stop there every time on the trip back. He says they are better than the ones the palace cooks make."

"Sweet mother of God," said Suarez. It was almost a prayer. "So you violated all our rules, all the procedures…"

"It seemed so harmless. And the boy, you know how he was…"

Suarez knew. Teo was so sweet, gentle, and generous, it was hard for anyone to refuse him anything.

He jerked upright. Then he dropped to his knees and grabbed Eduardo's bloody shirt in both hands. "What do you mean the boy *was*? Tell me what happened to him!"

"Let go of me and I will." Eduardo pushed himself up to more of a sitting position. "We parked near the stand. Gomez got out first to reconnoiter. The usual woman was at the stand. There were two men and three women nearby, eating cookies. None of them looked like threats."

"So how many of you got out and how many stayed with the boy?"

More silence.

"Don't tell me you let the boy go with you!"

"We had done it a dozen times! Nothing ever happened!"

"And each time increased the chance that someone would know your schedule. Eduardo, I am ashamed of you."

"I am too, Luis. Don't you know that?"

There was a knock on the cell door. "The doctor is here."

"Tell him to wait."

Suarez turned back to the prisoner. "So what happened?"

"We walked toward the stand. Teo ran ahead, excited. I heard a pop sound. Javier screamed. I turned and saw him falling and then it felt like something hit me in the neck. I tumbled to the dirt."

"You weren't shot."

"No. They had Tasers. Three of us went down instantly. Gomez is built like a bull. He tore the dart off, but before he could reach his gun one of the men kicked him in the crotch. While he was down, they shocked him again. Before we could recover, our hands were tied, and we had sacks over our heads."

"What happened to the boy?"

"I heard him screaming. While they were dragging us down, I heard our car start." Eduardo shrugged. "Gomez got loose and freed us. The whole village was empty. Our phones were gone so we couldn't call anyone. We had to walk to the next village."

"And that's where you phoned," said Suarez, "to tell us what happened."

"They said they had no phones there. And besides…"

"By then running away seemed like the best idea."

"Not getting caught was the best idea." He sighed. "I failed at that too."

"Yes, you did." Suarez banged on the door. "Come in, doctor. Make sure he doesn't die."

The doctor, a short and fussy-looking man made a tsk-tsk noise as he neared his patient.

"Meanwhile, Eduardo, think about the kidnappers. I will send someone in to get descriptions of them."

The prisoner nodded.

"And doctor, when you are done, stick around. We will need you for more casualties."

The doctor's eyebrows rose. "More? Has there been some sort of disaster?"

"There will be."

* * * *

"Lunch time," sang Alberto.

Teo didn't know what to make of this man. He seemed friendly. There was sadness under his smile. Sadness and so much anger.

And he kept saying horrible things about Papa. Or rather, he brought in other people and they said the things. The *lies*.

They had to be lying. Teo understood that his father had to be strong, had to do things people didn't like, but always for the country's good.

But there were so many people with so many terrible stories…

There was a knock on the door and Alberto opened it. A woman came in. Her face was concealed, but Teo was sure he would know the limp if he saw it again. She carried two plates, each covered by another plate. The smell was delicious.

"Thank you, my dear. Put them on the table," said Alberto.

She did and placed spoons beside them. She left without ever looking at Teo.

"Enjoy," said Alberto, cheerfully. "I know it isn't up to your standards, but it is the best we can do out here."

Breakfast had been fruit and a bowl of gruel. Teo was hungry. He lifted the lid and found roast chicken and rice, beans, and vegetables. "It's good. Why don't you eat?"

"Thank you, Teo. I will." Alberto lifted the plate. There was a small pile of rice, a smaller one of beans.

Teo stared. "You don't get chicken?"

"Oh, most people in this country don't get to eat as well as our rulers. We're lucky to get this much." Alberto nodded. "Don't let your food get cold, Teo. Children starve to death every night within sight of your palace."

* * * *

Hidalgo was at the ornate desk in his study, typing on a computer. He barely looked up when Suarez saluted. "Well?"

"It's not any of the usual terrorist groups or insurgents."

The president turned and fixed him with shrewd eyes. "And you know this how?"

"We keep a close eye on them. Even the ones hiding up in the mountains have contacts in the city. There's no movement, no chatter. If they were planning something—carrying out something—like this, there would be radio conversations. Families would have vanished."

"I understand." Hidalgo lit a cigar, gazing at the far wall.

Suarez felt a sense of relief. The great man was much more in control than the previous night. Like any leader he had grasped the situation and was moving forward.

"So what is your next move, Suarez?"

"We pivot. We change direction."

"Meaning?"

"We stop looking for the usual suspects and stretch the nets wider." He hoped that sounded like a strategy, and not desperation.

* * * *

Suarez slept in his room at the central police station, having neither time nor inclination to return to his home. Long after midnight a sudden thought hammered him awake and he sat up with a gasp.

Why?

That was the question they should be asking.

Having kidnapped the president's son, the plotters could have asked for almost anything.

All right, they didn't want money. But they could have demanded that Hidalgo resign. Hell, they could have told him to kill himself. Suarez didn't know how that would have turned out.

But instead they had ordered the president to record a list of the people he had killed. Why such a strange request?

Suarez ran his hands through his hair. All right, what would happen if Hidalgo was forced to resign?

Easy. As soon as he had Teo back he would return to power.

And if the kidnappers managed to convince him to commit suicide to free his son?

He would have been replaced by one of his colleagues, some member of the inner circle.

Now Suarez was beginning to see it. To the kidnappers, it was no solution for another member of the junta take power. Any of the leadership would be as bad as the current ruler.

But if Hidalgo's confession were made public, the result would not only condemn him but all of his chief supporters. Even the ones not implicated in the actual document would be damned for their association with such an evil man.

The international community would never let any of them take power; the stench of the public confession would forbid it. And many of the would-be leaders would be dodging indictments by the World Court.

He remembered one line he had read on the computer screen. *Suarez advised me to make an example of those campesinos.*

That was what the kidnappers intended. Not tormenting Hidalgo. Bringing down the entire ruling class.

And if Suarez didn't find a way to stop them, they might succeed.

He got out of bed, sleep forgotten. He called his office. "Borges? It's me. Send all our agents to the cafes near the universities. Get them listening for gossip there."

Somebody clever planned this, someone who wasn't in the files. But even the cleverest people have to talk to others, and some of those others talk too much.

* * * *

The break came at siesta time. "Chief, this is Morales. I may have something for you, I don't know."

"Tell me quick."

"I was in a bar on Calle Zapotero, a real dive. Just keeping my ears open. There was a guy bragging that he knew something about the president's family. He was drunk, of course."

"What did you do?"

"Called the patrol. Had him arrested for drunk and disorderly. He should be on his way to the lock-up now."

Suarez grabbed a pen. "Well done, Morales. What's the fellow's name?"

* * * *

It was Ricardo Aragon. By the time he had been rushed to the central station, bewildered and rapidly sobering, Suarez had memorized his thin file.

Aragon was a drinker, a petty scoundrel. Jailed a few times, but too lazy to commit any major crimes.

Had this nobody somehow gotten involved with the clever man, or was it another dead end?

"What am I doing here?" Aragon whined as soon as Suarez walked in. "Since when can't a man have a drink or two? I was—"

Suarez showed him a palm like he was directing traffic. "Ricardo, I know that you are very stupid—"

"How dare you! I have—"

Suarez slapped him across the face, hard enough to rock him in his seat. "If you need proof that you are stupid, there it is. You are arguing with a man who can drop you in an unmarked grave simply to save the paperwork it would take to jail you for the rest of your life. Please pay attention."

Aragon opened his mouth, then shut it again. He still looked angry, and that was no good. Suarez needed him frightened.

"For the love of God, Ricardo, please listen to me. Can you remember one time in your life, *just one single miserable moment*, when you made the smart choice?"

Aragon gaped.

Suarez leaned forward. "Think, man! Surely there was one golden opportunity in your pathetic life you didn't throw away. Am I right?"

A cautious nod.

"Excellent! Please, remember how that felt. I want you to feel that way again, right now. So don't speak until you are sure it is not your natural stupidity coming out again. All right?"

Suarez sat down with a sigh. "If you were being smart, you would know that you weren't brought to the Central Station for drunkenness. Something else must be happening. The smart part of you would know it is time to stop blustering and listen. Can you do that?"

Another nod.

"Good! Now, you were bragging in a tavern that you knew something about the president's family. What is it?"

"I never said—"

Suarez raised his hand and Aragon shrank back.

"Better! Please be smart, Ricardo.'

Aragon's face grew shifty. He thought he was being clever. "If I help you what do I get for it?" Then quickly, "That's a smart question, isn't it?"

Suarez nodded approvingly. "Yes. If you don't ask it too often. I regret, though, that the answer is that you won't get much. All I can offer you by way of reward is a worthless scrap of a thing."

Aragon frowned. "And what is that?"

"Your life." Suarez unholstered his gun, hefted it for Aragon to study—which he did, wide-eyed—and then placed it carefully on the table, within easy reach of the prisoner.

"If you aren't a coward, you can pick that up and shoot me, or better yet, use me as a hostage to escape."

"I would never make it out of here alive."

"You see? Already you are acting smarter. Now, tell me about the president's family."

"Alberto Junin."

He blurted it so suddenly that Suarez took a moment to realize it was a name.

"Who is— No. Wait a moment." He stood up and went to the door and gestured to the guard. "Tell Borges to look up Alberto Junin. I need everything, and I need it now."

He turned back to the prisoner, who was staring at the pistol with a mixture of fascination and loathing.

"So, who is this Junin?"

"He's the one you should be talking to, not me."

"Oh, I assure you I will. But who is he, exactly?"

"A school teacher from the eastern province. He's been living in the hills for at least a year. Last month he came to our village and asked a woman I know if there was anything she would like to say to the brat if she had the chance."

Suarez frowned. "And who is the brat?"

"The president's boy."

His jaw dropped in astonishment. To call Teo a brat was ridiculous. It would be like calling Hidalgo "the saint."

"Is that what Junin called him? The brat?"

"No. He called him the monster's son."

Ah. Now they were back in familiar territory.

"Why did he think this woman would be interested in Teo Hidalgo?"

Aragon shrugged. "When her son was thirteen, he went to the market for beans and rice one afternoon. He didn't make it back by curfew."

Suarez shut his eyes for a moment. "Was the body found?"

"On the town dump the next morning."

Instinctively, Suarez prepared to spout the usual story about insurgents attacking curfew-breakers, but neither of them would believe it, and there was no time for fairy tales.

"What did the woman say?"

"She said she would be happy to talk to the boy. One day last week, Junin came and took her away."

Suarez nodded. "And who is this woman?"

Aragon swallowed. "My sister."

"Does she live in your village?"

"Yes, but you won't find her there now." Again, the eyes grew shifty. "I should get something special for betraying my own sister, yes?"

"Absolutely." Suarez agreed. He picked up his gun and fired.

Aragon howled.

"You get to keep your other foot."

* * * *

The president didn't look up from the computer. "So who is this fellow Junin?"

"A school teacher from the east."

"And why did he not appear in the files I spend so much money on, the ones you keep on our nation's enemies?"

"He was there, sir, but in a closed file. We thought he was dead."

"Apparently not. How did that happen?"

"His school burned down. Many of the students died and we thought he had, too."

"Oh, God." Hidalgo looked up, shocked. Then he turned his face back down to the screen. "I forgot about the school burnings! If I had left them out, who knows what this madman would do to my son?" He typed furiously.

Suarez felt a sickness deep inside. "Sir, are you including stories like that?"

"All the deaths, Suarez! You heard the man."

The president was different. Suarez had heard that confession was good for the soul. Writing all this horror, letting it out in the open, seemed to be making Hidalgo almost giddy.

He paused. "So this Junin was a coward, was he? He fled and left the children to die?"

"We don't know, sir. This is the first hint we have had that he was alive."

"So what are you doing now?"

"Aragon's sister is hiding with her cousin in the village of Parma. I will go there and question her. General Ribiero has been told to prepare a raiding party."

"Excellent, Suarez. You are doing…" He frowned at the computer screen. "Those miners who tried to organize last year. Do you know how many really died? Borges can only give me the official number."

* * * *

"Why?" said Teo. "Why are you being so *mean*?"

Alberto frowned. He had walked into the boy's cell to find him lying on the floor weeping.

"I'm sorry if the dinner was not up to your standard."

"You know that's not what I'm talking about! Why are you telling me all of this about him?"

Alberto sat down. "You are an intelligent boy. It is time you knew what everyone else knows about your country's president."

"But he's my father!"

"He is indeed." The man sniffed. "I have been studying President Hidalgo for more than a year, ever since he burned down the school where I taught, with all the children inside. You haven't heard about that one yet. You see, he decided the schools in the hills were teaching radical ideas. So he decided to make examples.

"I happened to be visiting my home that day. My father was sick from too many years working without proper protective equipment in a coal mine owned by friends of your father. He's dead now."

Alberto shrugged. "Where was I? Oh yes, I came back to find the school gone…. Well, enough about that. You asked why I want you to hear all this."

He leaned forward. "This is what I concluded from my studies. The only person on earth your father cares about is you. You are the only one whose opinion interests him. He needs your respect."

The boy wiped his eyes. "And you want to make me hate him."

Alberto considered that. "No, not at all. It's people like your father who want to make people do things, feel things. I am a teacher. I want you to know the truth, and think about it, and draw your own conclusions."

He stood up.

"I think you have had enough for today. We will leave you alone until bed time. Think about what you have learned, Teo. This will all be over in a day or two."

The boy wiped his eyes. "I shouldn't cry. Men don't cry."

"Oh yes, they do," said Alberto. "When children die, men weep. I know this."

Teo was left alone again. He had been alone more in the last two days than in a whole year. There was nothing to look at in the room but the bookcase and that, he had discovered, was full of scrapbooks of articles from newspapers and magazines in other countries, all repeating the same sort of horrors Teo had been hearing in person.

The boy thought about all he had learned. And about his father, the warm and loving man he had known all his life.

And he kept thinking.

* * * *

Alberto Junin went down the hall to the room that had been the office when this old shell had been a thriving factory. Mendez was bent over his computer.

"Anything?"

Mendez shook his head. "No mail from the palace. And nothing on the official website. They still haven't admitted the boy is missing."

Alberto nodded. "He still has one day."

"Do you really think that bastard will send you a full confession?"

Alberto opened a suitcase full of medical supplies. "He will send something. He needs the boy in order to complete himself. But he will probably try to get by with a whitewashed version too, so we need to be ready."

"Ready for what?"

Alberto picked up a small surgical saw. "If we need to cut a piece off the boy to show we are serious we need to make sure there is plenty of anesthetic and antiseptics." He sniffed. "No point in being cruel."

* * * *

The next part went so easily it was an anticlimax. Suarez spent the night drive to Parma recalling all he had learned at the special anti-terrorist training he had received by the U.S. military. It hadn't been much, really. They gave him a sample and wanted him to go home and convince Hidalgo to send for more American advisors for his army. Hidalgo had seen no need.

Now the need was here.

Some of the G.I.s had shown Suarez what they called enhanced interrogation techniques. He was prepared to use them all to get answers from Marta Benitez and get them fast.

But it wasn't necessary. His men found her hiding in the field behind her cousin's house. They dragged her inside, where she glared at him, defiance coming out with every breath.

But all Suarez needed was one question. "Shall I ask you where Junin is holding the boy, or shall I ask Carlita?"

Carlita was her only living child, nine years old.

That was all it took.

* * * *

"Impossible." General Ribiero was sweating like a pig. "I cannot arrange a raid today. It will be a disaster."

"Are you saying you cannot rescue my son?" said Hidalgo. Suarez had persuaded him to move into his office for this meeting, away from the computer screen where he had been typing, typing for almost three days straight.

"Sir, this is the most important mission the army has engaged in for many years. We can't go in half-ready."

Hidalgo scowled. "How much time do you need?"

Ribiero swallowed.

He was stalling, Suarez thought. Hoping something would happen that would make his part unnecessary.

When was the last time Ribiero's army had faced anything more than unarmed peasants, or at worst, a few suicidal terrorists? When had he last gambled at high stakes?

Perhaps never.

"Mr. President," said Suarez. "You have important work to be doing. Let me confer with the general and we will give you a report soon."

Hidalgo was already heading back to his study. He nodded. "Yes. Quickly."

Ribiero gaped at Suarez. "What has happened to him?"

"His only son is in mortal danger. Do you think he is stone?"

But he understood what the general was saying; the president they were used to would never have let an underling leave him hanging like that.

"You need to have your men ready to attack in less than four hours."

Ribiero shook his head. "That is imp—"

"Did you see the computer in his office?"

A frown. "Yes. So?"

"The kidnappers have demanded he send them a confession of every killing for which he is responsible. If the boy has not been freed by nine o'clock tonight, he will send it to them. Tomorrow it will be news all over the world."

"That would be the end of him!"

"Of *him,* General? I assure you, he has included the details of the so-called Battle of Mariposa. The *true* details. How long will your career last after that story becomes public knowledge?"

Ribiero swallowed. "We will be ready in an hour."

"Excellent. I will be going with you."

"But—" He shrugged. "You must understand my men have no experience in operations in which we try to get anyone out alive."

"They have one hour to learn."

* * * *

Marta Benitez had told them that Alberto Junin had not taken the boy back the mountains. He had been more cunning than that. Instead, he ran his operation from a small village a few miles from the capital, in the rundown remains of a furniture factory that cronies of the president had closed down years before, to prepare for some purpose that had never come to fruition. The villagers, whose economy had never recovered, were not inclined to tell the police if they saw anything suspicious.

When General Ribiero announced that his hand-picked men were ready to launch the rescue mission, Hidalgo had torn himself away from his computerized confession and announced he was coming with them.

"You must not, sir."

"It's my son, Suarez."

"Exactly, sir. You are too emotionally involved. Besides, the soldiers will be torn, trying to protect you as well as Teo."

The president thought, then nodded. "I won't go into the factory, but I will go to the village."

Suarez noted he had brought a laptop with him, just in case the boy was not there. And, as always, a bodyguard, in case anyone thought about keeping him from sending the confession.

They set Hidalgo up in the town hall, imprisoning the mayor and his staff in a back room. No one would get out to warn the terrorists.

Ribiero had himself together at last. He explained that his best unit would come in the back door, closest to the room where they believed the boy was being held.

"I will be with the main force around the corner from the front door. As soon as we hear any action, over the radio or live we'll come in. But until you men run into trouble, it's your show. If you can get the child without firing a shot, so much the better."

Suarez insisted on going in with the crack force through the back. The dark door was reinforced steel, completely out of place on the dusty adobe wall. Suarez had assumed the men would force it with a ram or explosives, but they were determined to slip in quietly. It took one of the soldiers three minutes to get through with picks.

"We're in," Suarez whispered into his microphone.

The hallway was dark and dusty, long and narrow. According to Marta, Teo's room was behind the third door on the right. She hadn't known what was behind the other doors.

They passed the first one, and Suarez envied the silence of the soldiers, feeling like a clumsy packhorse by comparison.

The troops had almost reached their target when a door on the left side opened. An old woman flung it wide. She screamed. "They're here!"

And so Suarez fired the first shot in the raid. The woman fell backwards. He heard a flash-bang and knew the men had thrown it into the boy's room before charging in. He desperately wanted to follow them, but knew he had to finish what he started.

He ran into the room on the left, which was a long empty space. A warehouse? The factory floor?

There was a small, older man with glasses at the far end: the schoolmaster. Junin wasn't trying to run away. He was smiling and raising a long piece of metal, aiming it at Suarez.

Rifle, he thought, though the shape was odd. When it reached Junin's shoulder, Suarez fired and kept firing.

The schoolmaster dropped to the ground, bleeding from the chest.

Suarez ran forward. The apparent rifle had been a big church crucifix.

Suicide by cop, that was what his trainers in the United States had called it. Junin had made sure they couldn't torture him into naming any accomplices.

Not important. All that mattered was the boy.

As Suarez ran back to the hall his heart was pounding. If Teo wasn't there they would be worse off than before. If the boy were hurt, or worse…

There were soldiers standing outside the cell, weapons in hand. They looked excited, but not terrified as if something had gotten wrong.

He entered. A younger man lay dead on the floor, bleeding from a dozen wounds. A half dozen soldiers were crowded at the far corner of the room.

"What is it?" croaked Suarez. "Is the boy all right?"

They made way for him. Teo was backed up against the wall, eyes wide with terror.

"Get away from him!" Suarez shouted. "Back up! Guard the door!"

He leaned forward. "Teo, it is your old friend, Luis. You're safe now!"

The boy was still blinking. The damned flash-bang had left him blind and deaf. Or was he just stunned by it all?

"Teo—" He put a hand on the boy's shoulder.

Instantly the child slapped it off. "Don't you touch me! Don't touch me!"

My God, what have they done to him?

"All right, all right, Teo. Whatever you want. Your father is waiting for you. Shall I take you to him?"

The boy rocked forward and back, forward and back. Suddenly he straightened up. "Yes! Take me to him."

"Of course." Suarez nodded to the general. "Escort us."

They didn't stop to fetch cars. Instead, the men formed a ring around Suarez and the boy, blocking them from all eyes as they walked out of the front door of the building and down the middle of the street.

The few people out and about in the village gawked in amazement at the band of soldiers moving down the street, guns at the ready, crowded around Suarez and the boy.

Teo would not be hurried. He walked fast, but Suarez could not persuade him to run.

"Your father is waiting for you. He wanted to come with the soldiers, but he knew you would be safer if he stayed away. But he is— He is—"

Suarez ran down. The boy didn't seem to notice him at all.

They reached City Hall. There in the main chamber stood President Hidalgo, staring at his only son like a starving man at a banquet.

Suarez and the soldiers stepped away. The boy looked at his father and rocked forward and back again.

Hidalgo dropped to one knee and held out his arms. "My son, thank God you are safe! Are you all right?"

To Suarez, Teo's face seemed blank. No, not blank, rigid. His eyes were slits. He didn't move.

Hidalgo's eyes widened. "Teo, my God, what have they done to you?"

There was no love in that sweet face. "They told me how you have treated our people."

The president's outstretched arms wavered and dropped.

"You have been too easy on them," said Teo. He sniffed. "Tomorrow we will begin to fix that."

And then Hidalgo wept.

Robert Lopresti is the author of two novels (most recently *Greenfellas*) and more than seventy short stories. He has won the Derringer and Black Orchid Novella Awards, been nominated for an Anthony, and been reprinted in *The Best American Mystery Stories*. He lives in the Pacific Northwest and blogs at SleuthSayers.com.

THE LAST THING HE REMEMBERED

PATRICIA DUSENBURY

Mike had been hearing voices for a while, distant but getting closer. He opened his eyes, and the light blinded him.

"He's awake." It was Lacey's voice. "He blinked. I saw him. Mom, go get Jason."

Cautiously, Mike squinted one eye open. Lacey was in his face, grinning like she'd won the lottery. Surprise opened both eyes, the light hit him again, and he squeezed them shut.

"Too bright." His throat was dry, and it hurt to talk. The air smelled funny, antiseptic and stuffy both.

Where the hell am I?

"I'll turn off the overhead." Footsteps and a click. "There, is that better? Oh, Mike, sweetheart, you gave us such a scare." Lacey was back, leaning over him.

He reached to console her, and his elbow hit a metal railing at the edge of his bed. A tube ran from the back of his hand to an IV pole. Wires connected his body to a monitor beside his bed.

"What happened?" he asked.

"You were in a house that blew up."

"Our house?"

"Not ours—"

"Dad." Jason burst into the room, knelt beside his bed, and hugged him. Jason, the poster child for adolescent pain in the ass, was saying how much he loved him.

"I was so scared." Lacey wiped away tears. "At first you were unconscious, and then they kept you in a coma to give your brain a rest. They just moved you down from intensive care."

Mike tried to get his bearings. He was in a hospital. He'd been injured—badly, judging from his family's behavior. He wiggled his toes. They still worked, so did his legs, but his head felt funny. He checked it and discovered heavy bandages.

"How long have I been here?"

"Five days." Lacey's lower lip wobbled like she might start bawling any minute. Jason was back on his feet and looking awkward. Lacey's mother smiled tentatively.

"Get me a Coke?" he said.

"Mr. Patterson." A dark-haired man wearing a plaid sports coat approached his bed. "Detective Joe Garcia." He opened his coat to reveal a badge. "Albuquerque Police Department."

Police? Mike tried to sit up and pain shot through his head. The monitor beeped.

A nurse hurried into the room, glanced at him, and did something to the monitor. The beeping stopped. "Time to leave, folks," she said. "Our patient needs his rest."

Everyone but Lacey moved toward the door.

"You too, please, Mrs. Patterson. The family can come back this evening."

"He wants a Coke," Lacey said.

"Go on home, Lace. She can get it."

"We can't go home," Jason said. "We're in Albuquerque, living in a motel."

"Albuquerque?"

"Don't worry, Mr. Patterson, temporary amnesia is common with head injuries." The nurse pushed a button and the head of his bed raised. She held a paper cup to his mouth. "Water. It's the best we can do."

* * * *

Either he slept through the evening visit or there was none, because the next thing Mike knew it was morning. Sunlight peeped in around drawn curtains. Lacey snored softly in a chair flattened out like an airplane seat. He was still attached to the IV and the monitor. On the screen, green lines made regular patterns beside big numbers labeled with abbreviations he didn't recognize. He had vague memories of people doing things to him, poking and prodding and feeding him like he was a baby. Under the bandage, his head itched.

Someone knocked on the door, and Lacey stirred. A tall woman wearing a white coat entered the room.

"Good morning." Her tone was brisk.

Lacey sat up. "Good morning, Doctor Furman."

"Sorry to disturb you, Mrs. Patterson, but I'd like to examine your husband."

"I'll go get coffee." Lacey put on a robe, shoved her feet into slippers, and shuffled out.

"Let's sit you up." The doctor hit the button to raise the head of his bed and once he was up, introduced herself as Inez Furman, his neurologist. Her badge said University of New Mexico Hospital, Albuquerque.

"Mike Patterson." He held out his hand. "I'm having memory problems."

"You've suffered a traumatic brain injury; it would be strange if you weren't." She pulled a chair up beside his bed. "You remember your name. Can you tell me your birthday?"

"July 17."

"And the year?"

"1972. Have we had this conversation before?"

"Yesterday, but you're doing much better today." She smiled. "I'm going to tell you three words. Later I'll ask if you remember them. Okay?"

"Okay."

"Cat, water, tree. Got it?"

"Cat, water, tree," he repeated.

"Now, can you recite the alphabet?"

He could, and he could count to fifty, but when she asked what the three words were, he didn't have a clue.

"How about today's date?" she said.

He thought hard. The last day he remembered was June 11th. He'd had a dentist appointment. Lacey said he'd been out five days, which would make today... "June 16th."

The doctor shook her head. "August 19th."

"August?" Beside him, the monitor screen blinked. The numbers were changing.

"Don't worry. This is early times. Your recall will improve." She pulled out a small mallet. "I'm going to test your motor reflexes. Can you turn sideways and hang your legs over the edge of the bed?"

She tapped his knees and elbows, his feet and wrists; she asked him to look up and down, left and right, and follow a light with his eyes. When she finished, she told him his prognosis was excellent.

"Your intracranial pressure has been within a normal range for some time now." She pointed to the monitor where a line labeled ICP held steady.

"Was I in an accident?"

"You were in a house that blew up."

"My house blew up?"

"I don't believe it was your house." She stood. "The best thing for you right now is to rest. I'll check back later today."

"Wait a minute." She paused in the doorway and he said, "Will I ever remember what happened?"

"I can't answer that question. However, I can tell you that the closer an event was to the time of the injury, the less likely you are to remember it."

Lacey walked in as Dr. Furman walked out. She dropped a quick kiss on his cheek, grabbed her clothes, and went into the bathroom to change. A nurse brought breakfast, a respiratory therapist checked his breathing, and a nursing assistant put fresh sheets on his bed. Mike knew he wanted to ask about something, but he couldn't remember what. His eyelids grew heavy.

When he woke, a dark-haired man was sitting in Lacey's chair looking at him.

"Where's my wife and who are you?"

"Your family went out to lunch." The man held up a badge. "Detective Joe Garcia, Albuquerque Police Department. We met yesterday."

"Sorry, I don't remember. Don't take it personally. I've got amnesia."

"The lady doc told me. She also said things will come back."

"Why do you want to talk to me?"

"The explosion where you got hurt," the detective said, "someone else died."

"Died?" From the corner of his eye, Mike saw the numbers on the monitor flash 120, 125, 130. "Someone I knew?"

"You tell me. Does the name L. Bradley Loomis mean anything to you?"

He searched what was left of his memory and came up with nothing. "It doesn't ring a bell. Was there a gas leak?"

"Nope." The detective shook his head. "A bomb."

"Like a terrorist bomb?"

"More personal. His front door was booby-trapped." Garcia's eyes flicked to the monitor screen where the numbers continued to rise. "I can understand why you'd feel uneasy."

"Someone was killed, and I was there?" Mike felt more than uneasy, and this police detective watching him as if he was a bug under a microscope didn't help.

"You were in the house. You sure you didn't know Loomis?"

"I want someone else here when we talk. My wife."

"Fair enough," Garcia said. "I'll be back tomorrow morning. See if you can remember what you were doing in Loomis's house."

After Garcia left, Mike found a pen and pad among the stuff on the bedside table and began a list of things to ask Lacey, starting with, *What was I doing in Albuquerque?*

When Lacey returned, Jason and Carol were with her. Carol stopped in the doorway.

"I'd better not come in. After yesterday, the doctor said only two people in the room at a time."

Mike grimaced. His mother-in-law was always hanging around the edges, there but not there, like she was waiting for an engraved invitation. It drove him nuts. What difference did it make if she listened from the doorway or sat in the room and listened? Either way, he couldn't say what he wanted to say. Lacey handed him a tall cup.

"Chocolate milkshake, your favorite—at least it used to be."

"Thanks."

The milkshake went down easy but left him feeling stuffed. He dozed off. When he woke, Lacey was back in the chair, reading a magazine. She looked up.

"You're awake. Good. Dinner will be here soon."

"Where's everyone?"

"Mom and Jason went back to the motel. It has a nice pool." She sighed. "This has been really hard on Mom."

Mike doubted it—he and his mother-in-law were not each other's biggest fans. His skepticism must have showed because Lacey pressed the point.

"The last time she was in a hospital—my Dad's stroke—how could you forget?" She clapped her hand over her mouth. "I'm sorry, Mike."

"It's okay and I do remember." Lacey's dad had been kept alive by machines for a week before the doctors said he wasn't going to wake up. They were sorry, they'd done all they could, but he'd been without oxygen for too long. The next month Carol moved in with them. It was supposed to be temporary, but….

"I'm glad it's just you," he said. "There's stuff I want to ask. Like what was I doing in Albuquerque?"

"You were on a business trip."

That made sense. Reynolds had been wanting to expand into New Mexico for a while now, but last he remembered, it was still at the talking stage. That must have changed during his missing months.

"What are you doing?" Lacey said.

"Taking notes so I don't forget." He finished writing. "What about the guy who died? Did I know him?"

"You probably heard of him. His name was something Loomis. His company sold junk phones to a bunch of Navajo who got mad. It was all over the news."

An aide rolled in a tray with two dinners on it. Mike made a couple notes and put the list aside. When he finished eating, he went back to it.

"Tell me about the junk phones. Why would I care?"

"We got Jason one, and you felt so bad you bought him a new iPhone." She made a face. "Which we couldn't afford, but you said we owed him because you didn't listen when he said his phone was junk."

"Was I mad at this guy Loomis?"

"You and lots of other people. The police think an irate customer booby-trapped his front door." Lacey shook her head. "I can't imagine actually killing someone over a cheap phone."

"Watch the news and you see people killed for less."

"That's why I don't watch the news."

"Speaking of phones, do you know where mine is?"

"Back at the motel in an envelope with your wallet and stuff. The hospital gave it to me when I first got here." Her eyes filled with tears. "Like you'd never need it again."

"It's okay, Lace. The doctor says I'm going to be fine. I need to check a couple things, and I should call the office tomorrow."

"Mr. Reynolds says not to worry. Insurance will cover everything, and your job is waiting for you."

"That's not it. I want to know what happened. What was I doing there?" When he lay quietly, words and pictures floated into his consciousness, but they vanished before he could pin them down.

"I don't know, but there's no point fretting about it now. The doctors say your memory will improve. It has already. I can tell." She kissed his forehead. "I'm going to turn in."

He watched her push the chair horizontal and drape a sheet over it. "That thing can't be comfortable. Go back to the motel and get a decent night's sleep." She paused, and he persisted. "I appreciate your staying with me when I was out of it, but I'm okay now."

"No, you're not."

"I'm getting better by the minute. Go. Get some sleep. I'll be okay."

"You're sure?"

"I'm positive. And leave your phone. I'll give it back tomorrow morning."

"Okay." She handed him her phone. "It's already hooked into the hospital's Wi-Fi. Now don't stay up half the night."

"I won't."

After Lacey left, Mike used her phone to search for information about traumatic brain injury. Medical articles confirmed what Dr. Furman had said. He'd probably recover completely, which made him one of the lucky ones. Meanwhile, he could expect short-term memory issues, and he might never remember what happened in the days or hours before his injury. The suggestions for coping were things he already did—make lists, keep his surroundings tidy, always put items like car keys in the same place. Lacey teased him about being OCD, but those habits would serve him well.

Googling *Loomis cell phone* got more than two million results. The first non-ad was a YouTube video. He clicked on the link.

A dozen pick-up trucks rolled down a two-lane road. The background looked like high desert, but it was nowhere Mike recognized. The convoy turned into a strip mall and parked at the far end of the lot. Men wearing jeans and shirts, hats and boots, climbed out. The narrator, who sounded British, pointed out that "weaponry" was visible in the back windows of most trucks, but the people themselves did not appear to be armed.

After a quick conference in the parking lot, the men walked into a phone store. The end. The video had a cool feeling, like an old-time western, but Mike couldn't imagine why so many people had watched it. He searched again, this time clicking on news. The earliest article was dated June 17, six days into his lost memory.

Twenty-two Navajo had been arrested for laying siege to a store that refused to take back their defective cell phones. The store manager claimed to have been threatened by armed Navajo, which explained why the video was a big deal. The article referenced other videos, so Mike went back to YouTube.

The British guy, probably a tourist, had resumed filming when the Navajo went inside and lined up at the counter, waiting to be helped. Told their phones came with no warranty, they refused to leave without speaking to a manager. So far, no one had threatened anyone, but the gathering had attracted attention. Others started filming, and someone must have called 9-1-1.

Multiple videos showed four sheriff's department SUVs pull up in front of the store, their blue lights flashing and sirens screaming. In the final sequence, deputies hustled the handcuffed Navajo out of the store. The manager never did appear.

The story went viral, and an anonymous phone company employee posted a memo from L. Bradley Loomis, regional sales director. The memo acknowledged problems with the phones. It suggested lowering the price, making the warranty a separate purchase, and targeting sales to "price sensitive market niches." In other words, the phones were junk, but they could be sold to poor people who wouldn't spend extra for a warranty and would therefore be stuck with the defective phones. Problem solved.

A photo of Loomis surfaced and gave evil a face. It was Caucasian, pasty pale with close-set eyes, a self-satisfied smirk, and a scraggly little chin beard. Mike enlarged the picture and noticed the flashy diamond ring on Loomis's pinky, the big Rolex on one wrist and the heavy gold chain around the other.

Screwing people pays well.

Déjà vu sent a shiver up Mike's spine. He'd looked at that picture before, and he'd had the same thought. He'd been angry because he'd been sucked into buying his son a crap phone. He remembered taking Jason to buy an iPhone—the kid had been ecstatic. He closed his eyes and concentrated on Loomis. There was more to remember, but it was still out of reach. He clicked on another link.

Numerous people had recognized L. Bradley Loomis. Before joining the phone company, he'd been a loan officer at a shady mortgage bank. Back then, he'd called himself Luke Loomis, but it was the same person—no question. People didn't forget the SOB who arranged the mortgage that ended up costing them their homes when housing prices fell. And they didn't give a damn if it had been in the fine print all along.

Mike gritted his teeth. A mortgage from Loomis's bank had filled the gap between what Lacey's parents got for their house in Kentucky and what they paid for their dream home in Florida. Losing that home had killed Lacey's father. Literally. He was found unconscious with the foreclosure notice in his hand.

A nurse walked into his room. "It's getting late, Mr. Patterson. Do you need something to help you sleep?" She glanced at the monitor. "Your blood pressure is up."

"I've been reading the news."

"This will help you sleep." She injected something into his IV.

He wrote down as much as he could before the drug took hold.

* * * *

The next morning Mike remembered what he'd learned without looking at his notes. He really was getting better. He lay in bed and thought about Loomis and the greedy people like him who caused others such pain. Carol had been crushed by her husband's sudden death, and God knows, life had not been the same since she moved in. His den had become her bedroom, and privacy had gone down the toilet. Carol wasn't happy with the arrangement either, but she couldn't afford anything decent on her own, and he couldn't afford to help her out. Poor Lacey was caught in the middle.

A knock on the door announced the arrival of an aide bringing his breakfast. Detective Garcia was two steps behind.

"How're you doing, Mr. Patterson?"

"My wife isn't here yet, and I'm about to eat. Come back later."

"No problem. You eat and I'll talk. We've learned some things I want to share with you."

Mike forced himself to meet the detective's gaze. On the monitor screen, the numbers he'd figured out were blood pressure jumped, and one of the lines formed jagged spikes.

Garcia chuckled. "You might as well be hooked up to a lie detector."

"That thing measures stress. I was at the scene of a crime, and I don't remember what happened. Any sane person would be stressed." He took a deep breath. "I went on the Internet last night, reading about Loomis."

"Not exactly a nice guy."

"Have you seen the stuff online? Lots of people wished him dead. One joker suggested a Go Fund Me to raise money for a hit man."

"We read it all."

"You didn't see anything from me."

"No, but we found you in the victim's house, in his bedroom to be specific."

"I wish I knew what I was doing there."

"So do we, Mr. Patterson, and we have our suspicions. Do you recall anything about Loomis's neighborhood?"

"No, and I'm not answering any more questions until my wife gets here."

"Fine, no questions, but there's more to tell."

"Not now." He shoved a forkful of scrambled eggs into his mouth.

"Have it your way. I'll be back this afternoon." With a mock salute, Garcia left.

Mike pushed his breakfast tray aside. He turned Lacey's phone back on and searched *Loomis fatal explosion*.

The articles all said the same thing. Loomis had died instantly when he opened his front door and set off a bomb powerful enough to destroy the front half of the house. A second man was found in the master bedroom, unconscious beneath chunks of ceiling. It hadn't taken long to identify him. His wallet had been in his pocket, and a van he'd rented was parked nearby.

The Internet told him what had happened, but nothing told him what he was doing there or what role he had played. Why had he rented a van?

The morning session with Dr. Furman was brief. He remembered the three words. She checked his reflexes and said he was making good progress. Lacey arrived soon after Doctor Furman left.

"It's just me," she said. "Jason is sleeping in, and I didn't want him to wake up alone, so I asked Mom to stay with him. They'll be here after lunch."

"No problem." He pointed to the chair Dr. Furman had vacated. "Come sit by me."

"How are you doing?"

"My memory is improving, but there are still big gaps. Do you remember me saying anything about renting a van in Albuquerque?"

"You were there on business."

"I know, but why did I rent a van?"

She shrugged. "I bet your office would know. Why don't you call them?"

"I would if your phone wasn't almost dead. I should have asked you to leave the charger."

"Darn. I meant to bring your phone, but I forgot all about it. I can go back and get it."

"Don't do that." He reached for her hand. "Look, Lace, I know this last week must have been hell for you. Why don't you give yourself a day off? Go shopping and get yourself a new outfit. I'm better, and they're keeping me busy with tests and therapy sessions."

"You sure?"

"Absolutely."

"I'll be back in time for dinner."

Lacey left, and he reread his notes. His memory was returning, and as Dr. Furman had predicted, the days furthest from his injury were coming back first. So far, it was bits and pieces, nothing coherent, and some of them felt ominous. The question about the van hovered, unanswered, in the back of his consciousness. It was still there that afternoon when Detective Garcia walked in.

"Where's your wife?"

"She went shopping. You should have come sooner."

"First I'm too early, then I'm too late. Sort of like Goldilocks." Garcia chuckled. "Do you remember that story, Mr. Patterson, Goldilocks and The Three Bears?"

"You wouldn't think it was funny if it was your memory gone to shit. I'm not answering any questions unless my wife is here."

"No problem. I'm telling, not asking. The Doc says you're making good progress. Maybe something I say will jog your memory. If I were you, I'd want to remember."

"I do, but I don't want you planting false memories."

"I'm after the truth, Mr. Patterson, and as I told you this morning, we've learned a lot." Garcia leaned forward. "Now, you and I were talking about Loomis's neighborhood."

"You were talking about it. I don't remember being there."

"It's very tidy. There was nothing on the street except your van, no cars in the driveways except what's left of Loomis's. We're talking suburbs, and the only motor vehicles in sight belong to the people who were inside a house that exploded. Strange, wouldn't you say?"

Mike willed himself to stay calm and ignore the damned monitor. He'd learned worrying made the numbers climb and slowing his breathing brought them down.

"So we ask the neighbors, and we find out parking on the street or in your driveway is against the homeowners' association rules."

"You can't park in your own driveway?"

"Nope, and if your kid leaves a bike lying in the yard, they'll confiscate it. You have to pay a fine to get it back."

Something clicked. He'd been looking at a computer in a library, at a street view that showed no cars or kids' toys, houses but no sign of the people who lived in them. He took a deep breath and checked the telltale monitor. His blood pressure was up and one of the lines formed jagged spikes. Garcia could see it too.

"A penny for your thoughts, Mr. Patterson."

It was another staring contest, and again, Mike was the first to look away. "I wouldn't want to live there."

"Me neither, and I couldn't afford it." Garcia folded his arms across his chest. "Now given the rules, you'd expect Loomis to park in his garage and enter the house from the door between the garage and the kitchen. You want to guess why he didn't?"

"I don't have a clue." This cop was playing cat and mouse with him, watching the monitor the whole time. Mike wanted to rip the damn wires off his body.

"Someone stole Loomis's garage door opener out of his car. It happened that morning when he was in court. He reported it to the Mattox police, but they didn't put two and two together until yesterday. You ever been to Mattox, Mr. Patterson?"

"No, and I don't know anything about explosives." Relief brought a smile. "I don't know how to build a bomb."

"There are instructions on-line, and you do know how to use the Internet, but let's stay with the vehicles. You were driving a rented van. Right?"

"That's what the newspaper said."

"According to the rental company, you specifically requested a white van. Do you remember why?"

"No, I don't." And he wished to hell he did.

"We asked your boss about it. Here's what he said." Garcia took out his phone, tapped on it a few times then held it up. "We videotape everything these days. Can you see okay?"

"Uh huh."

A disembodied voice, not Garcia's, was asking questions. Reynolds confirmed that Mike Patterson was employed by Reynolds Restaurant Supply and had flown to Albuquerque on company business.

"We're expanding into Albuquerque and Santa Fe. Mike was scouting out potential customers."

"Do you know why he rented a van?"

"He had to rent something, and it was a chance to see how a van handled." Reynolds rubbed the back of his neck. He looked uncomfortable. "We supply restaurants with everything but staff and food. Back in April, one of our vans turned over on a sharp curve. The driver wasn't hurt, but we lost all the contents, thousands of dollars' worth of crystal and china. Our insurance paid, but they're going to drop us if it happens again. Mike wanted to see how a standard van handled on mountain roads."

"There's more, but that's the gist of it." Garcia tapped the phone and the video disappeared. "Anything ring a bell?"

"I remember the accident." There was no sharp curve. The other vehicle had run a red light. Their insurance paid because the other driver had no insurance—no license either.

"I'm getting tired," he said. "Let's wrap this up."

"Almost finished," Garcia put his phone back in his pocket. "How about the problem with the insurance—do you remember that?"

"No." Sweat prickled his armpits. He didn't dare look at the monitor. "But that doesn't mean anything."

"It might mean your memory is improving. You don't remember because it didn't happen. We talked to your insurance agent. You lied to your boss. Why?"

Numbers flashed, lines spiked, and the monitor beeped. A nurse hurried into the room and shut down the beeping. She glared at Garcia.

"You've been warned not to upset Mr. Patterson. I'll have to ask you to leave. Now." She frowned at the monitor. "Would you like a sedative, Mr. Patterson?"

"No thanks." He slowed his breathing. "Just peace and quiet. No visitors except my wife."

Garcia paused in the doorway. "I'll stop by tomorrow. The doc says they expect to release you in a couple days, and I don't want you going back to Phoenix before we finish talking."

Mike stared at the ceiling. Garcia was right; he'd lied to his boss. He'd done it to justify renting a van. He didn't remember actually renting the van, but he remembered planning to, and he remembered why. The insurance adjustor had given him the idea, which meant she might have told the cops. They'd been discussing the accident and she'd suggested, only half joking, that Reynolds Restaurant Supply repaint their vans.

"Anything but white," she'd said. "Painters, electricians, delivery services, everyone drives a white van. They're everywhere, so no one notices them. This is the third accident I've worked this month involving an invisible white van."

He had plenty of reason to hate Loomis, but did Garcia know? Had Lacey told him about Jason's phone? What about her parents' mortgage? Had she even made that connection?

* * * *

Lacey walked in carrying a shopping bag. Smiling, she held up a lacy nightgown.

"This is for your welcome home party."

"It's pretty." He forced an answering smile and asked if she'd talked to Garcia. "Other than in front of me."

"Once or twice."

"What have you told him?"

"About what?"

"About me. About our family."

"I don't know—nothing much."

"What kind of nothing much?"

"Just nothing much. Why are you yelling at me?"

"I'm sorry, Lace. That detective keeps asking questions, and it gets under my skin because I don't know the answers. I don't know what he knows."

"Who cares what he knows? You have nothing to hide."

"I was in Loomis's house. They found me unconscious in his house." *How could she fail to see the problem?*

"You know what I think?" She didn't wait for an answer. "I think you were nearby and heard the explosion. Maybe you saw it—I don't know. No one else was around, so you ran inside to make sure no one was trapped in the house. That's the kind of person you are. That stupid policeman needs to stop bugging you. I'm going to talk to the doctors about banning him from your room."

"Don't do that. It's okay, Lace. It really is."

Her expression said things were far from okay. She folded up her new nightgown and put it back in the bag. He felt like a jerk.

"I'm sorry, Lace. I'm in a crappy mood—nothing to worry about, it's part of the recovery process—but I'm not fit company. Go back to the motel, check in with Jason and your mom, catch a movie."

"The doctors say you'll be able to come home in a couple days."

"I'm going to get out of here, and we'll be fine. I love you." He hoped they'd be fine. It was far from a sure thing. "I'll see you tomorrow."

Lacey painted him a hero, but she was wrong. He'd stalked Loomis on-line, and he'd gone to the library to do it so there would be no record on his computer. He'd rented a white van in order to be invisible—at least inconspicuous—and gone to Loomis's home. That was not the behavior of an innocent man. He didn't know how to make a bomb, but he could have found instructions on-line.

Who am I? He buried his face in his hands. *What have I done?*

* * * *

The answers came in the wee small hours when a noise in the corridor roused him from deep slumber. Suspended in the hazy space between awake and asleep, he remembered—not everything but enough to know he was not the man his family thought he was. He was not the man he'd hoped to be.

How much did the cops know? Garcia had mentioned talking to the neighbors. Someone's security camera could have caught him. People who lived there would have outdoor cameras. It was that kind of neighborhood.

The clock on the TV said 4:47. He had a little over an hour before the morning nurse would come to check on him. After that, it would be one person after another, poking here and prodding there, asking questions and demanding his attention. He pulled out his pad and reviewed his notes. He had a little over an hour to devise a story the police might believe or, even if they didn't believe, could not disprove.

* * * *

Garcia showed up soon after Dr. Furman came through on her morning rounds.

"Is your wife here yet?"

"No, but we can talk anyway. I've started remembering things."

"Mind if I tape our conversation?"

"No problem." He waited while Garcia pulled out his phone and set it to record. "The last thing I remember was picking up the van. I really did want to see how a van handled, although it had nothing to do with the accident. I planned to drive up to Santa Fe and work my way back down to Albuquerque, checking out restaurants along the way. I had reservations to spend the night here. At the Colonial Hotel. You can check with them."

"That's a pretty specific memory," Garcia said.

"I'm a detail person—my wife would say compulsive."

"Your boss said you crossed every t and dotted every i."

"That's my job."

"The killer was a careful planner," Garcia observed. "He knew when Loomis would be in court."

"I don't know anything about that," Mike lied.

Garcia pointed to the monitor where the blood pressure numbers were rising. "You sure?"

"You just implied that I conspired to kill someone. Of course I reacted." He couldn't imagine killing anyone—not even a scumbag like Loomis. But if he'd been asked yesterday, he would have sworn that he'd never steal. He took a slow breath, and the numbers stopped flashing.

"You don't remember driving to Santa Fe?" Garcia said.

"No." He hadn't driven to Santa Fe. He'd gone directly to Loomis's house. "Nothing after renting the van."

"Did you read about the trial?"

"Not yet."

"The defense moved to allow videos taken by witnesses. The prosecution objected. The judge said they were admissible, and that was the ball game. I can't come up with the technical term, but the judge threw the charges out because they were bullshit."

"Sounds right."

"The trial ends, Loomis goes home, and boom he's dead." Garcia held his gaze. "I work homicide, Mr. Patterson. We're willing to overlook your venture into B&E—that's breaking and entering—particularly since you have no criminal record and didn't accomplish anything but getting yourself blown up."

Mike looked away. Garcia was right. He'd broken in. He'd walked around to the back and forced the patio door. He'd convinced himself stealing from Loomis was righteous, like Robin Hood. Take from the rich and give to the needy. What's more, Loomis got rich by cheating people. Someone at Loomis's company—maybe even Loomis himself—had cost Lacey's folks their home and her father his life.

He'd told himself he was also a victim. Living with his mother-in-law was driving him crazy. The money from pawning Loomis's jewelry would make the down payment on a unit in that assisted living place Carol had been eyeing. Everyone would live happily ever after.

Garcia cleared his throat. "We have the guy who stole the garage door opener from Loomis's vehicle. We explained that he could be charged as an accessory before the fact in a homicide." He smiled. "Let's just say he's cooperating with our investigation."

"Then why are you here?"

"Because you were at the scene of the crime. Timing says you might have seen the man who planted the bomb, seen his car. Juries like eye witnesses, although between you and me, they're unreliable as hell."

"I can't help you."

"Are you sure? Confession is good for the soul."

"Confessing what?" Lacey stood in the doorway, her hands on her hips. "He didn't do anything wrong, and you need to stop bothering him."

"Lacey." Mike started to tell her everything was okay, but then he saw the bag in her right hand. She'd remembered his stuff, and he remembered the rest.

The monitor came to life. His blood pressure had shot up, and he didn't need a machine to tell him that his heart was pounding. He took a long slow breath, another one. He closed his eyes and prayed.

"Well, Mrs. Patterson, it looks like your husband is very glad to see you." Garcia hauled himself to his feet. He reached in his coat for a business card and laid it on the bedside table. "If you change your mind, Mr. Patterson, give me a call."

Lacey shot a dirty look at Garcia's departing back. "I don't like him."

"He's just doing his job."

"Your belongings." She put the bag on top of Garcia's card.

"Thanks."

He pulled her down for a kiss, and his other hand checked the bag. His phone and wallet were inside, along with two rings. One would be his wedding ring. The other would be a diamond pinky ring. He'd found it and a bunch of gold chains in a leather box on Loomis's bureau. The last thing he remembered was slipping the ring onto his finger for safekeeping. First chance he got, he'd drop it down a sewer.

Patricia Dusenbury's first novel, *A Perfect Victim*, won the 2015 Electronic Publishing Industry Coalition award for best mystery. The sequels, *Secrets, Lies & Homicide* and *A House of Her Own* were finalists. Her short stories have appeared in anthologies and E-zines. "Cold Turkey," published in *Flash Bang Mysteries*, was a Derringer finalist.

PAINT THE CLOWN RED
LAIRD LONG

I stopped Kurt Kincaid as he tried to slip through the doorway into Bonhomme's 'art' room.

"What's the meaning of this?" the lanky cat burglar complained, elegantly dressed, as usual, in a camel hair coat, tux and tails, and a wine-colored silk scarf.

"I'm working for the fat man tonight," I said. "Protecting his 'investments'."

"From his friends?"

"Exactly." I knew in advance the rogue's gallery that Cyril Bonhomme had invited to his home for the grand unveiling of his latest art acquisition.

Kincaid huffed indignantly, as I searched him up one side and down the other, pulled a black leather case out of his tuxedo jacket pocket. "What have we here?" I snapped the case open, gawked down at a brilliant ruby necklace, the gems dangling off the gold chain like red liquid teardrops.

"*That* is the Beaumont necklace," Kincaid stated. "It, uh, recently came into my possession, and I thought perhaps Mr. Bonhomme might be interested in purchasing it. We've done business in the past, you know."

I knew. I also knew about the Beaumont robbery, from what I'd read in the papers. But I wasn't there to prosecute felonies, just protect the fat man's property. So, I snapped the case shut and stowed it back into Kincaid's pocket, gave him the thumb-through into Bonhomme's art room.

"Hold it right there, Minto!" I barked, bodily blocking entrance to the sawed-off, shifty-eyed black marketeer who had appeared out of nowhere.

"Make way, gumshoe!" he growled.

"I thought you hated Bonhomme's very ample guts, Minto, after he outbid you on that lot of World War I Iron Crosses? Why're you even showing up here?"

"Because Saul Minto and I have business to discuss, that's why," the great man himself answered, suddenly looming over my left shoulder. "I have some items for Saul to, uh, move for me—on the market."

I shrugged, went over the runt with a fine-tooth comb, finding nothing more incriminating than some flaccid balloons he claimed to have brought along for the occasion as a joke. His insider knowledge of the "market" had obviously tipped him off as to what lay in store. I waved him on through.

"Ah, good," Bonhomme bellowed in my ear, "we're almost ready, Clive. Come, come!" He waved a puffy hand at the thin man weaving his way down the hall towards us.

Clive Stanton nodded, his jade eyes shining with more than just greeting. He had a bottle of red wine in his right hand; a pewter flask in the breast pocket of his suit jacket, I found out when I frisked him. The man was one of the top art forgers and book dust jacket counterfeiters in the country, and he'd done jail time when he'd tried to sell the fat man a doctored *Great Gatsby* first edition. But he was the forgiving type, with the right wine.

"In honor of the unveiling!" he now shouted, holding up his bottle of wine. And then the flask when I handed it back to him, after having sloshed it around to my satisfaction. I was there to confiscate guns, knives, brass knuckles, burglary tools, and photographic equipment, not liquid inspiration.

"You going to search me, too?" someone murmured.

Bonhomme dragged Stanton inside his roomful of treasures, and Dawn Dunoir stood where the artful forger had.

Dunoir was an art restorer of some renown, returning dirty, damaged, and dilapidated *objets d'art* back to their original glory. Rumor was she wasn't above hiring some down-and-outers to help her out when business was slow, by deliberately defacing valuable artwork which she then lent her delicate touch to restore, at an indelicate price.

She was an object of rare beauty, herself, but that didn't stop me from patting her down like a pickpocket. I double-checked her giant tube of red lipstick and jar of red nail polish.

"A woman can never be caught without her cosmetics," she murmured, floating past me on a cloud of perfume.

Bonhomme broke out the fine crystal goblets and distributed everybody but me a handsome portion of Stanton's gifted red wine. Then he ambled over to the far wall of the room, where a red velvet cloth was draped over his latest acquisition. The group followed after him, expectantly.

"Friends," he declared, without irony, "I've invited you all here to be the first to view what may be my greatest art discovery yet—*The Clown*

Prince of Antwerp!"

Some gasping and much jealous grumbling greeted this pronouncement. I watched all and sundry like a hawk.

"Believed lost forever during the Napoleonic wars, through endless searching, and much 'persuading', I have at last secured and authenticated that missing masterpiece of the Flemish great, Hugo Von Rinn, and will unveil it here for the first time in public since 1809."

Bonhomme paused, puffed up to almost twice his normal gargantuan size, gripping the edge of the velvet covering. "And now, Dawn, if you wouldn't mind handling that spotlight, while my agent, Mr. Wallace, mans the room lights…"

Dawn Dunoir sashayed back to the fat man's huge desk on which he'd set up a baby spotlight aimed at the painting thirty feet beyond. As I walked back to the door where the light switch was located.

Stanton drained his wine glass, thoroughly, glancing back forlornly at the bottle sitting on the desk next to Dunoir. While Kincaid nervously fingered the breast pocket of his tux. And Minto impatiently snapped one of his balloons.

"Lights, Mr. Wallace!"

I flicked off the lights, plunging the room into total darkness.

Velvet rustled, and Bonhomme croaked, "Spotlight, Ms. Dunoir!"

There was the sound of fingernails fumbling on metal. Then a splashing sound. And then the spotlight beamed forth, illuminating *The Clown Prince of Antwerp.*

"No!" Bonhomme wailed, his moment of triumph turning to tragedy. "It's ruined!"

A red liquid splattered the crying clown with the painted-on smile.

I flicked the room lights back on, yelled, "Freeze!"

They froze. Dunoir by the desk, Stanton and Minto ten feet in front of the painting, Kincaid even closer, Bonhomme beside his desecrated artwork, and himself. "I told you to lay off the cheap theatrics," I chided the fat man, moving quickly over to the group.

I inspected the tableau up-close. Kincaid's wine glass was empty, Stanton's exhibiting a trace of red liquid, Minto's full. There were some red dots on Kincaid's camel hair coat, on the lapels and on the collar at the back. The color matched the stain on the painting.

I waved Dunoir over. "What was splashed on the painting—wine?"

She closely inspected the liquid obscuring the clown's face, carefully touched it, tasted it. "Unfortunately," she passed judgment, "it's red paint, not red wine. You're going to have a dickens of a time getting that out,

Bonhomme." She smiled pleasantly. "But if I can be of any service…"

The fat man's jowls quivered with rage. "One of you vile creatures destroyed my masterpiece!" he roared. "And one of you is going to pay!"

"How can you put a price on beauty?" I stated blandly. "But I bet you'll give it your best shot, Bonhomme."

I turned to the group of four guests. "So, get out your checkbook, touch-up-artist, and start making with the pen and ink figure drawings."

Bonhomme thundered, "Who did it!?"

"It's the work of Clive Stanton," I replied, fingering the artless forger. "His flask was actually filled with paint, not alcohol, which he poured into his empty wine glass when the lights went out and then tossed at the artwork. I'd noticed that he'd thoroughly drained his glass of wine just before the lights were doused, yet when they came back on, there was a small amount of red liquid in his glass—a small amount of leftover paint.

"Kurt Kincaid's coat lapels are dotted with red paint, because he took some of the backsplash when the liquid splattered against the picture, being the one of the four closest to the painting. He's also been splashed on the *back* of his collar, however, eliminating him as a suspect. He could've only been splashed that way if someone standing behind him had tossed the liquid.

"And Saul Minto's wine glass is still full, meaning he didn't toss any liquid at the painting. And Dawn Dunoir was the one furthest away from the painting, thirty feet away—well out of accurate liquid-tossing range," I concluded matter-of-factly.

Stanton made a dash for the door, out of the frame. But I hung a foot on his ankle, spilling him onto the floor. Bonhomme then scraped him back up and directed some fisted criticism at the blank canvas of the man's face. It was no masterpiece, but we all appreciated it nonetheless.

✗

Laird Long pounds out fiction in all genres. Big guy, sense of humor. Writing credits include the magazines *Blue Murder Magazine*, *Sherlock Holmes Mystery Magazine*, and *Pulp Literature*; stories in the anthologies *The Mammoth Book of New Comic Fantasy*, *The Big Book of Bizarro*, and *New Canadian Noir*; and the standalone book *No Accounting for Danger*.

THE CONTAGIOUS KILLER

BRYCE WALTON

CLASSIC REPRINT

Originally published in *Alfred Hitchcock's*
Mystery Magazine, January 1966.

I chased more wild leads all through another hot July day and got back to the squad-room late and depressed. The case was going badly for me, but I had done all I knew how to do. The pressure was starting to build up.

The air conditioning was out again. The squad-room was sticky and smelled like a stale cigar. A few other boys stopped typing reports and mumbled embarrassed greetings. Someone even said "Hi," then hesitated before adding "Lieutenant," as if it were an uncertain afterthought. I hung my jacket over the back of my chair, rolled up soggy shirtsleeves and checked the memo spike on my desk. Nothing, as usual, but negative reports; and a note to call my wife. My boy, Jamie, would forge into the act. He would ask, "Dad, how come you haven't solved the murders yet?"

I could tell him what I'd been telling the reporters for a week, that I expected a break in the case any minute now. But kids, especially Jamie, know you're lying as soon as you open your big mouth.

I called the Bureau of Criminal Identification to see if they had turned up any sex criminals we hadn't questioned yet. They had not. I called Miller to see if he'd finished another check-through of cab company trip sheets; always a chance some cabbie might remember some suspicious character in a vital pickup or let-out area. Miller had nothing new. I called to see if the pictures sent to the girls' home towns, to firms they had worked for, to schools they had attended, had turned up anything. They had not. I called Morelli to see if any anonymous tips had come in worth investigating. None had. I called Hoppy to see if he'd turned up anything by dragging all the flophouses again. He had not.

Then I just sat there feeling that frightening sense of failure and helpless anger. The truth was, I had to admit, I had a "cold case." When women are killed on impulse by a psychopath, you have to get a strong lead on a suspect within twenty-four hours, or it ices up and you may be years nabbing a killer; or you never do. The killer isn't usually acquainted with his victim. Probably he's never seen her before, has no personal connection with her other than some sudden sick compulsion. That eliminates all ordinary motives or leads, and there's no other way to connect this sort of murderer with the victims than through eyewitnesses and/or very obvious clues left by the killer. My killer hadn't left witnesses or clues. All he'd left lying around were the parts of his two dismembered victims, two young pretty girls who had come to the city to live a more exciting and glamorous life, but who had gone bad; the sort you see walking along the honky-tonk streets looking for adventure.

I felt an itch along the back of my neck, about where the axe would fall. It was my first big murder case since being made lieutenant, and it would likely be my last. Not that I'd get fired or downgraded. I'd be shoved down the hall to the clerical department as a typewriter jockey or a public relations stooge. No thanks, I wouldn't care for that.

The phone rang and I had the sinking feeling even before I picked up the receiver that it was the Chief.

"Get up here on the double, McKenna," he said.

The Chief's air conditioner worked just fine, but that office felt like an airless mousetrap to me. Our Chief is a heavy, intense and practical fellow who has few ideals and is very conscious of politics. He doesn't waste time or words and he didn't waste them now. He said, "Someone else is being put on your case, McKenna."

I felt numb, and for a minute I couldn't say anything. Then I said, "Well, all right, I'll see you around." I turned and started to walk out.

"Don't be stupid, McKenna. Just wait and listen a minute."

I turned. "It won't do any good. I've done all that anyone can do."

The Chief twisted his hands nervously. He blinked at me uneasily. "Just cool down a minute, McKenna, and listen. I know you've done all anyone can do; at least, all that any ordinary mortals around this precinct can do. But this is something special—a sort of weird, way-out thing. And I want you to listen. First, get this clearly, McKenna. Bringing this other guy in isn't my idea. It's the D.A. He's crazy for a quick arrest and conviction. It's his business, it's political. Our business is to do what we're told, and to remember that the D.A. is the mayor's nephew. Okay?"

"Okay," I said.

"Ever hear of an ex-cop name of Steve Blackburn?"

I shook my head.

"You were transferred to this precinct after Blackburn left," the Chief said. "But he was a lieutenant here too, in homicide. One day he found himself in charge of a butcher murder case, three women and a psycho. A case much like yours, McKenna."

He hesitated and gave me a funny squinting look. "In fact, according to Blackburn, it *is* the same case. He's convinced the D.A. that it's the same killer making a comeback."

I didn't care to say anything. I waited.

Finally the Chief went on. "This means a lot to Blackburn. His case was about a year and a half ago, and his killer got away. The case froze over. Blackburn was hit hard. Seems he was wrapped up in this case. It was like a fever. He couldn't think of anything else. Month after month he refused to do anything but hunt this psycho. For over a year he devoted all of his time to this obsession. That's what it got to be—an obsession. He says he learned everything about the killer.

"He studied pathological crime until it was running out of his ears. But the guy disappeared. He didn't kill again. Blackburn had learned so much about the psycho he had a trap laid for him, but the guy didn't kill again, so Blackburn lost him. Blackburn kept saying, 'If he'd only killed again I would have nabbed him.' Anyway, to tag a long story, Blackburn was so obsessed with this thing that when he lost it, he couldn't stand the gaff. He hit the bottle too much, and finally he had to leave the force. It was all an ugly business."

"Blackburn's being put in charge now?" I asked.

"No. The D.A. has brought him in as a special consultant," the Chief said. "After all, if it is the same killer, Blackburn's way ahead of us."

"But what if it isn't the same killer?" I said. "What if Blackburn is, like you say, obsessed? What if he just has to come back to try to prove something, make up for his failure?"

The Chief laced his fingers together and pretended he was having trouble pulling them apart. "Ours not to reason why, McKenna. The point is, officially you're still in charge. Blackburn's not on the force." The Chief took a deep breath. "Anyway, Blackburn is certain he's right. Know where he is now? He's cruising in a police car down on South Main where the killings occurred. He says the killer will strike again. Tonight!"

"Tonight," I said. My mouth suddenly felt dry.

"That's right," the Chief said. "You're to take a car down there. Meet Blackburn at the Third and Main parking lot at six-thirty."

The unmarked patrol car rolled into the parking lot at exactly six-thirty. I walked over. There was a hot haze of smog that stung my eyes. Blackburn had a dark lean face that looked out at me like a vulture's. He said in a quick nervous way, "You drive, McKenna. That's your name, isn't it?" I nodded and he slid away from under the wheel. "You drive now. I want to look and get the feel of it again." He turned and looked out the opened window of the cruiser. "It's like getting in the mood again, McKenna. You get the beat and feel of a killer, and this is his street. This is Joe's street. You know it is."

"Joe?" I said.

"About the only thing I didn't find out about him was his name," Blackburn said. "I call him Joe."

"Where to?" I asked.

"Just cruise slow. Up and down Main."

"How far up and down Main?" I asked. I turned out of the lot into the traffic.

"Between First and Eighth," Blackburn said. He wore a dark suit, a dark tie, and he had black thinning hair speckled with white. He was in his forties, but had a dried-out look and his skin was as tanned as leather. He kept his head out of the window most of the time and sniffed like a bloodhound.

"No hard feelings I hope," he said to me once.

I shrugged. "It doesn't matter."

"Sure, you resent me coming in, McKenna. Don't blame you, but I had to do it." His voice got low and tight. "But don't worry, you'll get the credit. All I want is Joe."

"That's the important thing," I said, with effort. "To get him—get him before he kills again."

"No," Blackburn said softly. "The most important thing is that you should never get filed away in the books as the guy who let a big one get away."

He paused. "I'm not here to prove anything, or get back at them. It's too late for that. All I want is to finish that job. I just want to get Joe. I want to finish it for good and go home."

"Where's home?" I asked.

"San Fernando. I have a little dairy ranch out there." He looked out the window as I cruised easily along the street, and the neon lights went on, and the all-night shooting galleries and hot dog stands and bars and strip-shows and all-night movie houses lit up. "Don't worry, McKenna," he said. "Whatever we do, you say you did it. This is strictly personal with me."

After another block, he touched my arm. "This is going to be a rough night probably. You have any questions before it starts?"

I thought awhile. "How do you know—I mean how can you be so sure it's the same guy?"

"What little they had about it in the papers added up," Blackburn said. "Then I dropped into the police lab and checked. All the other clues were the same, especially those police photos." Blackburn chuckled, but I couldn't say what kind of humor it was, if any. "The public likes gore, but the dirtiest sensational sheet in the country could never publish pictures like that."

"I guess not," I said, to continue the conversation. The memory of those cheap rooms where Joe had done his work was bad. I'd been broken in to all the sordid stuff by serving my time with the Black Maria squad, but those two murder rooms had been too raw for my taste. Even the memory of them made me queasy.

"Take the gin bottles," Blackburn said. "You found two empty gin bottles. Well, there always was. In my three cases there always were two empty gin bottles. It always took him about ten hours to do a job, and all the time he was locked in the room using his knife on them he would be taking nips of gin. In both of your cases there were two empty gin bottles, right?"

"Yes," I said.

"And didn't the autopsy show that in both your cases the entire operation covered about ten hours?"

"Give or take a few minutes," I said. Blackburn's eyes were brighter now, and his voice was edgy with excitement. It was a very warm night but I felt a chill go down my arms.

"Same brand too," Blackburn said. "King's?"

"That's right," I said. "King's Gin."

"I know him, you see, McKenna. And every one of his kills are the same. Every detail is the same. With these psychos, murder is a ritual. I've read about all there is on the subject. It's part of a cycle, a repetition syndrome, as the books say. Everything in the ritual must always be exactly the same. In some, the cycle is longer than others. But this pressure builds and builds, and finally they have to do it. A ritualistic act, McKenna, and each Jane is what they call a live fetish. Each Jane is the same Jane to this Joe, always about the same age and looks. And everything Joe does just before the murder and during it is a strict repetition. That's how I know."

"But how can you know he'll kill again? Here, tonight?"

"He has to kill three of them," Blackburn said, "always three. I didn't know that before, you see. I set a trap and waited, but he'd already filled his quota and he didn't turn up again. But now I know there has to be three, and I know how many days apart the jobs are spaced. You've had two so far. There has to be a third. The time is tonight."

"You knew he would come back?" I said.

"Nobody could know that," Blackburn said, "but I knew he'd come back if he were able. Things can happen to a psycho. Sometimes they get better and don't need the ritual anymore. They have split personalities. They can be fairly respected guys in some community, maybe with a family. They get this psychotic pressure and they go off somewhere—usually to the same or a similar place—and get rid of the pressure. Then they go back home and are good members of the community until the urge seizes them again. It goes in a regular cycle, so I figured if he ever repeated again, it would be here." His voice had risen and now had the taut sound of a stretched wire. "I've waited and waited, McKenna, and I insisted that the D.A. let me have one more chance at butcher boy. I had to convince him. You think I'd miss this chance?"

"I don't think so," I answered.

"Pull in there behind the station wagon," he said. We got out and Blackburn took a deep breath as if he enjoyed the smell of South Main, the sour feverish smell of that wild street on a hot Saturday night. "Let's walk, McKenna."

We strolled past the dark doorways under cheap signs saying rooms $1.50 and up. About every other entrance went into a dim bar with juke music beating out over the street, and girls perched on bar stools looking out into the dusk like hungry owls.

We strolled on through a dizzy glare as more midway neon blazed on. We walked past the sparkling jukelights. Sirens whined. A screaming woman was dragged out of a doorway by two uniformed cops. A bearded man, barefoot, sat on a curb, laughing softly. The air was ripe with the smell of chili, pizza pies, and stale beer.

Then it turned damp and misty and a thin drizzle fell under the blinking neon. Blackburn led me back down the west side of skid row, past the recreation palace and the girlie shows.

Once he stopped and stood looking up silently into the mist. I looked up and realized with a shiver that it was one of the cheap rooming dives where the second killing I was investigating had occurred. "You see, there's always the liquor store within a few doors, and within one block there's always the monster show." He pointed.

At the corner I saw the marquee of the horror movie, and I heard

Blackburn say in an odd, tight voice, "Come on, McKenna. We have to get the mood of it. We only have a few hours."

We stood in front of the all-night, two-bit movie house which specialized in a triple horror bill. The teasers out front were life-sized cardboard cutouts of monsters, each holding in his arms a scantily clad woman whose mouth was painted a bright red, always open and fixed in a silent scream. The huge cutouts seemed to be leering and offering these screaming women to the pedestrians walking by, some of whom seemed to be secretly wishing they could accept the monsters' offers.

Blackburn said in almost a whisper as he stood close to me, "Take a good look, McKenna. You'll start to get the feel of it and of him—I mean Joe. See, the monsters and their Janes all look pretty much the same too, in a way, just like it is for Joe, and every movie is a ritual killing someone experiences vicariously."

"You sure have thought about it a lot," I said.

"For years," Blackburn admitted. "Is there much difference between Joe and the rest of us? A difference only in degree, McKenna. Every guy who enjoys this movie feels like our boy Joe, a little. It isn't so hard to see what this pressure is that builds up in Joe. You can feel it and so can I, and everybody else who will let himself do it. And that's how you catch guys like Joe. You have to identify with them as much as possible. I'm going to catch Joe because I've thought and studied, and I can be. Joe. I mean, I know enough about what makes him tick—"

"I get the point," I said quickly.

"Good, that's fine. I'm glad you're getting it, because if we work this through to the finish, you've got to get in the mood."

"I'm getting into it now," I said.

A wino jostled us. Blackburn gave him a disgusted shove and he fell flat in the gutter.

We kept looking at the gorilla-man, wolf-man, and tattered mummy handling those silently screaming women. Characters kept ambling along and stopping and looking, and some of them kept looking and moistening their lips. It occurred to me that any one of them might be Joe.

Blackburn had gotten change out of his pocket and was stepping toward the ticket-seller's booth. I grabbed his arm, and he turned around slowly and looked at me for a second as if he had never seen me before.

"What's up now?" I asked.

"We're going to see the show. This is where it starts."

"I saw these shows years back," I said.

"Not the way we're going to see them now, McKenna. This is the first step." He paused and rubbed the flat of his hand across his thin mouth. "You see, this is where Joe always goes—before he does it."

I had to take a deep breath. "How do you know that?"

"Ticket stubs. Didn't you find them, too, McKenna? In those rooms, there must have been ticket stubs, from this particular theater?"

I felt a drop of sweat run down the side of my face. "Yes, there were. But they couldn't mean anything. The ticket seller here, the usher and ticket taker admitted hundreds that afternoon. They couldn't recall anything, or anybody unusual. The tickets could have been anybody's. They just don't add up to anything, so I don't see how you can tell."

Blackburn gave me a thin smile. Under the neon in the dark mist, that smile looked like a twist of black wire. "Five murders, and in every room a ticket stub from a local horror movie is hardly coincidence, is it, McKenna? In fact, every one of those killings was in a room rented within a block of a house showing these creep pictures."

"So how do the creep pictures figure in it?" I asked.

"Gets Joe in the mood," Blackburn said softly. "You can see how that is, can't you? Forget everything else, the way I do, and try to think like Joe thinks. You sit in the dark and look at this and you're all alone, sort of secret-like in the dark, watching this stuff, and you identify with it and start getting stirred up. It's part of the ritual, sort of like those war dances the Indians used, to get themselves worked up and in the mood. Come on, let's go in, get in character."

He bought the tickets and we went into the lobby, which had a stale, suppressing smell of wine, stale smoke and beer, sweat; the smell of skid row bottled up on a wet summer night. We stood there and Blackburn was breathing quickly. He moved over toward the center aisle and looked down it. I heard growls and screams from the screen. Empty bottles rolled in the dark somewhere. A few guys were snoring, their heads propped up skillfully on their hands. Bums scrounged a nickel here and another nickel or two there, and came in here to get a little sleep. They knew enough, though, to keep their heads from wobbling so the usher and the cops wouldn't notice and give them a whack and kick them back out into the wet night.

"It's about the fifth row from the front, in the center," Blackburn said. "Those seats are empty. That's where Joe sits."

"You couldn't know that," I said, "what row and seat he sits in."

"Just about," Blackburn said. "I worked it out very carefully with an optometrist—several of them in fact. I know how tall he is too, and his build and the color of his hair. I've run lab tests on all that, strands of his hair, his skin, which we find under the fingernails of the Janes, and this all adds up to—"

"But how can you tell where he would sit in a movie?"

"One of the Janes broke his glasses, McKenna. We found part of the broken lenses. Couldn't trace the manufacturer, but we went over the lenses and figured out the exact degree of astigmatism. You can figure just about exactly where he sits. But the important thing is the mood, McKenna, the feel of it."

An usher with slumped shoulders, pimples, and a greasy uniform jacket came up and said, "You got to keep your voices down."

Blackburn looked at him like he was something pinned to a board. "Get out of here, boy," he said. The usher blinked and said it again. I showed him my wallet with my identity as a police lieutenant, and my badge. The usher backed off and Blackburn gave him a push. "Get lost."

Blackburn looked at his watch, then at the screen. "I've checked the show times. Joe usually starts working on the Janes about two a.m. He goes right up to the room from the movie. He's already got the Jane up there, drunk, or already too hurt to get away. He watches the horror pix, gets himself worked up to just the right pitch, then walks straight out of here to the room and goes to work with his shark-killing knife. That's an odd one, isn't it? The shark-killing knife. I never figured out where he picked up one."

"How do you know it's a shark knife?" I asked.

"We figured the length, breadth, thickness of the blade, also the sharpness. Also I got an isotopic analysis of the steel from particles in the bone. It's a shark knife, all right. Let's sit down."

Another movie started. My eyes ached, from straining at the screen and from the smoke-filled air. The smell was bad, too. I kept imagining I was inhaling about ten million germs a second. Six horror movies had gone by. And it was hot in there, but I kept getting chills up and down my arms.

I wasn't discriminating by this time. The monsters all looked alike, and the women being dragged away to a hideous fate, their clothes mostly ripped off, screaming and screaming, all looked alike to me, and their screams sounded the same, all phony and unconvincing. But the shadowy faces around me were absorbed in it. They sat there, their eyes wide and sort of glazed in the reflecting light from the screen.

"I figure this is about it, maybe another twenty minutes or so. It's nearly one-thirty. That means Joe's big hypo scene has to be coming up in about twenty minutes. Just keep a straight face and wait. I'll give you the sign. I'll squeeze your arm."

"Then what do we do? If we grab him, what about the woman?"

"What does that mean?" Blackburn asked.

"I mean," I said, "that according to your theory, Joe's already got the woman up in the room. He's already done some work on her, or tied her up. She has to be waiting when he leaves the movie here, all worked up and in the mood for it. So what if he gets shot, or gets away, or just won't tell us where the woman is?"

Blackburn stared at me, his face pale in the light from the screen. I don't think he'd considered the woman at all until then. "Oh, yes, sure. Well, I'll give you the sign, and when he goes out of here we'll tail him."

I nodded. We waited. Then Joe came in.

Blackburn squeezed my arm, and I rolled my eyes a little and my headache went away. Joe stood at the end of the row on the aisle, and he wasn't anyone you would single out to be much different than the rest of us. I couldn't tell the color of his hair, nor see that he was wearing glasses until he turned his face toward me, but somehow I had the feeling I would have known anyway that it was Joe. Maybe I was in the mood by then. I'd seen enough monster stuff to last me a lifetime. I had the beat, the feel of it.

I watched Joe out of the corner of my eye as he moved in and sat down just to my right. Only one seat separated us. He leaned back and braced his knees against the back of the seat in front of him. He sighed. Later—I don't know how much later but it was the longest period of my life—he leaned tensely forward. He put his hands on the seat in front of him and his head moved. It kept moving back and forth, and I saw the light shining on his glasses.

Blackburn had timed it within a few minutes when Joe would get up and leave the theater. We followed him. He went into a liquor store. He bought, I knew, two fifths of King's Gin, and came out twisting the sack and hurrying through the mist. A raincoat flipped, and thinning hair and glasses glinted in the drizzle.

We followed him to a dark entranceway under a sign that said rooms $1.50 and up. He hesitated, then ducked in there. I had a raw edgy feeling and a nasty taste in my mouth as Blackburn opened the door and looked up the stairs. I could hear his sharp quick breathing. When he turned and grinned at me his eyes had a shine like dark glass.

"We're wasting time," I said.

"We have to give him a little time too," Blackburn whispered. His eyes glittered with excitement.

"Listen," I said, "there's a girl up there. God knows what's happening. We've got to get up there."

"We've got time," Blackburn said. "First the drinking, the gin, remember. He has to work up to it."

"We've got him now," I said. "Let's go up!"

"Easy," Blackburn said. "You want to break the mood?"

"What's the matter with you?" I asked. "Who cares now about mood?"

The night man at the fleabag's closet-sized lobby told us the man we described as Joe had rented 307. I followed Blackburn up there. He was moving fast, then he started taking his time again, going up the stairs like he was suddenly tired.

The third floor hall was like a yellow cave. It smelled of stale grease and disinfectant and cockroach powder. Blackburn stopped and bent down and stuck his ear carefully against the door of 307.

I heard glass clinking in there. I heard a grunt and a sigh, and something like a moan in there. I could feel the sweat running down my face. I released the spring clip of the holster under my jacket and got my .38 out into the open. I touched Blackburn on the shoulder. He didn't move.

"Let's go in," I said, very low.

He didn't look at me. His body was rigid. He didn't seem to be breathing. He had his ear tight to the door and he was staring.

I heard other sounds then. Something in my stomach seemed to turn completely over. "Let's go in now," I whispered. He held up one hand for me to be quiet. He didn't look up at me. I heard those sounds again. I dug my fingers into Blackburn's arm. It was supposed to be his show. But what was he doing just listening to it?

"Blackburn?" I said.

He didn't move. He just squatted there, listening, and I heard a quick excited wheeze in his breath.

"I'm going in," I said.

His hand came around and touched my wrist. It was cold. It shivered a little. He whispered, and his eyes were pleading. "McKenna, wait! Give him a few more minutes. You can see how it is—I mean after all this time—you have..."

I saw how it was all right. I felt a moment of real horror. I saw how it was in his eyes—that glint of excitement.

"He's going to kill her," I said.

He gripped my arm and his mouth turned hard. "What does it matter?" he whispered. "Know what I mean, McKenna? You know? I mean, listen, some little chippie who will end up on a slab anyway, what does it matter now? Think about it, you'll see. You just don't feel it enough to know."

I felt his cheekbone slide under my swinging fist. Then I hit the door with my shoulder. I hit it again. I could feel Blackburn's hands dragging at me, and I kicked him in the face to get him off me before I got a shark knife in my belly.

The girl was too drunk to care much about whatever had happened so far. Joe looked at me through his thick-lensed glasses in a weird way, as if I had interrupted a study period in a dormitory. Then he came at me with his ten-inch hunting knife. I shot him.

When I went back out to go downstairs to call, Blackburn was on his knees. He was looking into the room and saying over and over, "Joe, Joe"—as if he had lost his brother.

✗

Bryce Walton (1918-1988) began his career in 1945 in the pulp-fiction field with stories in numerous science fiction magazines. As he matured and mastered his craft, he switched to mysteries, and over the decades published hundreds of short stories in the leading magazines of the day. Wildside Press is working to reprint all of his short fiction.

www.ingramcontent.com/pod-product-compliance
Lightning Source LLC
Chambersburg PA
CBHW050827180626
46814CB00004B/1502